Crime Scenes

Amy Lockett

Published by Trellis Publishing, 2021.

CRIME SCENES

First edition. July 5, 2021.

ISBN: 979-8224814848

Written by Amy Lockett.

CRIME SCENES

AMY LOCKETT

Chapter One

He'd spent five years in that hellhole before he made an informed decision: prison fucking sucks. He spent the majority of his day locked in a cell with some psychopath that claimed to hear voices in his head telling him to do crazy shit like wear his underwear on his head or punch that big guy, Stone, in the yard. Stone had nearly killed the poor bastard, but Joe Sullivan, aka "Sully" here, didn't give two shits about him. Not when he ate something gray that might have once been meat for breakfast, lunch, *and* dinner and drank water with a yellowish tint to it. Not when he slept on mattresses lumpier than the alley floors he used to sleep on as a kid, when his mother was jobless and they had no place to call home. Not when he had these assholes who call themselves correctional officers screaming in his ear like they're talking to some old deaf guy and shoving him around like it's some kind of game.

So many times he's wanted to retaliate, to bash their heads in, to slit their throats with a handmade shank, to slap their own cuffs onto their wrists and beat them mercilessly with their own nightsticks. But he was smarter than that; he knew that were he to so much as pluck a single hair from any guard's head, there would be consequences. Namely, more time added on to his sentence and even harsher punishment from the dickheads within the prison itself; the very same ones that were supposed to be protecting him from his other cell mates.

But the very worst part about all of this shit was the fact that he hadn't even done anything wrong to deserve it—well, at least not what they *thought* he'd done.

He's not going to lie; he's wasted a few traitors to the gang. More than one man is buried six feet under with his trademark cigarette burn on the back of the neck, but he swears on his mother's grave that he never even went near that chick they're saying he offed. He didn't even recognize her name, but apparently she was some rich bitch daughter of a senator or something. Raped and killed and dumped in an alley about a mile away from his house, a cigarette burn on the back of her neck and a threatening letter—supposedly from him—found in the pocket of her designer coat.

The police had barely even had to prove his guilt. He was so well-known in this city, by all the jurors and the deliberation had taken less than a minute before he was found Guilty of all crimes. He was sentenced to 20-Life and sent upstream. His girl, Pat, visited him sometimes and they used Morse taps to communicate as they chatted about mundane subjects like the weather and sports games he couldn't give two shits about.

Through their taps, he found out about the man who framed him, Rick Silas, who'd once been his friend, but was now a bitter rival. Rick and Joe had had a falling out years ago over something as absurd as splitting their shares from a lifted purse. There was only about a hundred dollars in the damn thing and Rick's argument was that, since he's the one who distracted the old lady in the first place, he should get a bigger split. Joe fought that it should be equal, since they both did their part in the theft. They'd fought like animals afterwards and one sock in the jaw had Rick backing off.

"Keep it, you greedy fuck!" he roared. "I'll find my own!" It had been a year until he saw Rick again and by that time he already had his own operation going. And Rick was never one to let go of grudges easily.

Cops starting inexplicably hanging around Joe's house, where he, Pat, and their own group of 'outlaws' lived. They sold drugs, stole drugs, used persuasive tactics—such as wielding a knife or a gun—to get their own way, and sold knockoffs. With the cops watching their place, Joe had to be ten times as careful, warding off the fuzz with his natural charm and power of persuasion. He fucked more than one female cop while Pat gave blowjobs to the majority of the males. They weren't bothered at all until the rich bitch turned up dead.

When the cops came to his door then, they didn't even ask questions before shoving a warrant in his face and slapping cuffs on him. At the time, Joe had no idea what he'd done or who had accused him but he already swore revenge as they shoved him into the back of a police car. Nobody wanted to listen to him plead his innocence and his trial was set for the following month, at the senator's insistence.

To find out that it was Rick was no big surprise, but he cursed out loud nonetheless, causing two of the guards to look his way.

"It's supposed to rain tomorrow," he lied and they looked away, uncaring.

It was then that he started to plan his revenge, meeting with Pat every few weeks to tap it out. She informed them that half of their guys had gone over to Rick's side when Joe went away, that they were now loyal to him and they were missing half of their manpower. Nobody had discovered the drug ring, but people were wary about buying from them now that their leader was away. Rick had done all of this, the prick. He would pay.

Now it was five years later and still there was no way to put their plan into action without Joe there to guide them. Pat was persuasive, but she was no gang leader, that was for damn sure. She was just his right hand; the person who echoed his orders and pointed a gun at whoever wavered. She was loyal and tough, but not tough enough for what he had in mind.

He was being driven insane every single day as he listened to his roommate mutter to himself, his head banging a rhythm against the wall. The only thing that kept him going anymore was the thirst for revenge. And Ann's letters.

Ann was another rich bitch. But she hadn't known the victim too well, except for the rumors she heard about the girl's tryst with some gang member. She was the first to write to him and tell him that she believed he was innocent. She wrote, in her first letter, that the gang member the girl was associated with was black, not white like Joe, and lived on the other side of the city—at least according to the rumors she'd heard. She'd tried to tell the cops that but none of them had listened. As far as they were concerned, she was just another little heiress looking for attention.

But the fact that somebody outside his own group thought he was innocent was enough to make Joe respond to that first letter—and then every letter thereafter. Their correspondence lasted for the entirety of his time in prison and he kept every single letter in his pillowcase, smiled when they crinkled at night as he rolled over. He didn't tell Pat about the letters.

He received one on the day his plans would be set into motion.

"Dear Joe,

Since receiving your last letter, I've been thinking a lot about what I would like to do for the rest of my life and I've decided that I'm going to go for it. I'm going to tell my father about my art, show him my paintings. Maybe he'll understand, you know? Maybe he won't be mad at all. I mean, I'm his daughter and he loves me, doesn't he? Won't he just be happy that I'm happy? I'm sure he will and so I'm going to tell him. Better late than never, after all. Right?

And Joe, I don't think I've ever asked you want you want to be. As in your career? I know it'll be a while before you can even consider it, but what is it that you've always wanted to do with your life? Something besides a life of crime, I mean, though to each his own I guess. Let me know in your next letter. I'll be looking forward to it.

Sincerely, Ann Martin"

It was shorter than most of his letters but he tucked it away into the inner coat of his jacket anyway. He would answer no more letters but he wouldn't leave them here, where psycho could get his hands on them. And, besides, having them closer to him made him feel safer as he made his way into the yard, where hundreds of other inmates stood, talking and just taking in the short amount of fresh air they were allotted each day.

Joe strolled casually through the crowds, down a familiar trail, his eyes skating over the faces of guards and his fellow inmates, many of whom were watching him. Platt, a lifer whose cell was located three down from Joe's gave him a hard glance and Joe smirked, held up two fingers, and walked further down the path, approaching the fence. He stopped and sat on the ground, closing his eyes as he counted backwards from a hundred and twenty. At five, his eyes opened again, just in time to see Platt punch Linster in the jaw. This was followed by Brown, another inmate, who sat with Joe at most meals, kneeing some unknown Latino in the groin.

Joe watched as the entire yard dissolved into chaos. The guards all around the yard ran straight towards the mess of inmates fighting one another, throwing punches and kicks and attacking one another with clawed hands. He smiled and reveled in the beauty of it before turning on his head and continuing down the path. Nobody even looked his way.

At the edge of the yard, about a quarter mile away from the entrance into the prison, there was a weak spot of fence. It wasn't electric, for safety reasons, but barbed wire ran all over its length and height—except here. Here, there was a noticeable gap in the barbs, where they split and were easily moved away to reveal a hole in the fence itself. When Joe had first noticed it, after taking a few laps around the sparse yard, there had been no way he could fit through it. It was too small even for the slender Pat to fit through.

But five years, fifty pounds less, and a bit of digging with a hundred or so easily broken plastic spoons, and the hole he made just underneath it might allow him a not-so-easy exit. This was his only chance at escape, either way. He had traded all his belongings to Platt and Brown for their little stunt. Platt didn't take too much convincing but Brown wasn't a lifer and had demanded almost more than Joe could give.

It proved worth it when Joe got down on his knees and slid through the hole like a slithering snake. Maybe he'd lost more weight than he thought in that shithole. He'd have to find a way to make it back after he got settled and wasted that dirtbag of an ex-partner, Rick.

He stood, brushed himself off, and then ran, never looking over his shoulder. The street was just a few hundred yards away and Pat would be waiting for him there, her trunk already open for him to jump into, a bag of fresh clothes for him to change into. She always had him covered, his Pat.

By the time he reached the car, he figured they must be looking for him so he wasted no breath to say hello or thank her for what she was doing. He just jumped into the trunk, shut it, and rolled around as she drove off. But he didn't really care about how sore his muscles were or what a close call he might have just had because he was free.

He was finally fucking free.

Chapter Two

There was absolutely no way they could return to his old house. For one thing, that would have been the first place they looked for him, and for another...well, since his incarceration and the whole operation going belly up and everything, they'd been forced to sell it.

"We got everything out, though," she told him as they walked into the new safe house, located about twenty miles from the city, in the middle of a large wooded area. It had belonged to Pat's late father, used only for fishing and cheating on her mother with his skanks. "It's all here, in the basement. The boys are out on the streets with it right now."

"How do they get back and forth?" Joe asked, always worried about his boys. He tugged his jeans up his hips; they were too big for him now.

"I drive them," Pat told him. "And Jimmy's got a good car now, too."

"Jimmy's sixteen," Joe snorted, looking around the tiny, damp living room.

"Not anymore," Pat said, tugging his hand as she moved towards the couch. "He's got a girl and a kid now. He's got a job down at the docks."

"And he's still selling?"

"He's still loyal. Besides, he ain't making enough to support his family with that dock shit; he needs the cash so I try to help him out, you know." Pat pushed him down onto the couch and climbed up onto his lap, smiling down on him like the Cheshire cat. "Let's not talk about it now, though, alright? We got more important things to do." She began to press kisses against his neck, smiling against his skin as he planted his hands on her hips.

"Pat, babe, we shouldn't—" he started but she pulled back and placed one finger against his lips to silence him.

"We've got plenty of time to do other shit, Joey," she said, "but you've been locked up for half a decade; surely there's something you missed in that time, huh? A bit more, uh, *pressing* issue." She palmed him and he groaned. "See? Now just sit back and relax; Patti's got it all covered, baby."

He was too distracted to argue further.

They lay in bed after three full rounds of what could barely be called sex. It was more like Pat had pounced on him, doing 90% of the work while he just lay there, reaping the benefits. The bed in the master bedroom was ten times as comfortable as the old prison mattress and he found himself starting to drift off as Pat lay against him, catching him up on everything that had happened since their last prison visit.

"...and he got that Martin girl all tied up somewhere in his house. Also, Jimmy's girl is pregnant again with a—"

"Wait," Joe interrupted. "What did you say? About the Martin girl? You mean *Ann*?"

"Yah, I think that's 'er name. Why? You know her?" Pat asked, looking up at him.

Joe nodded as he sat up, dislodging Pat. "Yeah," he said. "she, ah, wrote to me. In prison."

"She's one of *those* chicks?" Pat laughed. "Crazy ass women fallin' for convicts who'd sooner kill them than—"

"You sayin' I'm a murderer, Pat?" Joe barked, startling her.

"'Course not, Joey," she assured him. "I mean, I know you killed people, but those bastards always had it comin', didn't they? So it's all good. I'm just saying *she* didn't know that, is all."

Joe took a deep breath and rubbed the back of his neck. "I know what you're sayin'," he said. "But Ann didn't think I was guilty. She said I must've been framed 'cause I didn't match the description of the girl's boyfriend. Apparently, he was in a gang too."

"Did she say which?" Ann asked, sitting up to rest on her knees next to him.

Joe nodded. "It was Rick's, obviously," he said. "We know that. Poor girl was probably lured in and murdered in cold blood."

"Not before they got their way with her I'll bet," Pat huffed. "Poor...what was her name again?"

"Something Grant, I don't fuckin' know," Joe sighed. "Point is, he killed that poor girl just to get back at me and now he's gonna kill Ann, too. 'Less we do somethin' about it."

"Which we are," Pat reminded him. "In just a few short weeks, we're gonna infiltrate his place and—"

"We don't have weeks, Patti," Joey growled, throwing the sheets off of his legs and standing. He grabbed his boxers and began pulling his clothes on. "We don't even have a few days. You know Rick; he'll play with his new little toy for a few days and then he'll get bored, shoot her dead, and bury her in the backyard." He shook his head. "I've seen him do it too many times and I ain't about to let another girl die on my account."

"So what do you wanna do, then?" Pat asked, following him out of the room, a sheet wrapped around her naked body. "Just storm in there with no backup *tonight*? He's got a million guys in that house of his; ain't no way we're gonna take them all down, just the two of us."

"He won't be keeping her in his house, anyway," Joe dismissed. "He's too smart for that. 'Specially since that girl's daddy is probably lookin' everywhere for her right at this very moment. No, he's keepin' her somewhere, but wh—" His eyes widened as he looked back at Pat. "Is Sabretooth still around?"

"You mean Rick's bitch?" Pat snorted humorlessly, shaking her head, dirty blonde locks shaking with the motion. "'Course he is. But you don't think…" Joe grinned. "Rick wouldn't keep that girl with Sabe; he's a twice-convicted rapist. He couldn't expect the perv to resist somebody like that."

"You said it yourself; Sabretooth is Rick's bitch; whatever he says, that dumbass does. Rick probably distracted him with a couple dozen of his own hoes, anyhow." He paused to take a breath. "Where's he livin' now, Sabretooth. He still got that house on Seventh?"

"Far as I know," Pat said. "I haven't spoken to the bastard in years, but I don't really see any reason for him to change his address; he's been out of jail eight years now. Supposedly, he's doing good, despite more allegations coming up on the contrary." She shook her head. "Even if Sabe *does* have the Martin girl, do you know how hard it's gonna be to bring down all *his* goons? We're gonna need at least a half dozen of our guys and I don't think they'll be up for something like that tonight, babe."

"First light, then," Joe said. "We'll leave when the sun rises; make sure everybody's got their shit together."

"Sweetheart," Pat replied, "I'm loyal to you; you know I am. But I ain't no miracle worker and those boys haven't had their shit together since they was in diapers."

Chapter Three

By morning, all but three of Joe's main group of men had arrived back to Pat's safehouse. Jimmy, Sam, and Teddy were all family men now, which surprised Joe but he wasn't about to take them away from what they'd all worked so hard to gain.

Besides, even without them he still had more than a dozen guys ready to help him take Sabretooth down. Sabe had been one of them once, before Rick had betrayed them all. It hadn't taken the bastard a week to pack up all his shit and run to Rick's side, though. Joe hadn't even been surprised—nor did he care, considering Sabretooth was a lousy shot and proved to be a double-crosser, anyway. Who needed him?

Thankfully, all the men that stayed knew Sabe well enough to know all his tells and his strengths and weaknesses and how fucking dumb that man got when anything in a skirt showed up. He thought with his dick and that was a fatal flaw that made Joe burst into random bouts of laughter. His boys followed.

The plan was simple: Their three strongest—Bo, Gabe, and Devon—would lead the group. Being the muscle meant that they'd be able to easily take out any shitheads guarding around the house and allow the rest to get in. Behind them were about six of Joe's most weapon-savvy men; TJ, Mart, Steve, Bardy, Paulie, and Fisher. Their weapons were, for the most part, concealed by their clothing, but easily accessible when they needed them. They would enter the house before Pat, Joe, and the rest, guns blazing as they took out anyone on the first floor (though they were warned to be way of any blonde girls who looked as if they might be scared or mistreated.) Once they cleared, Joe and Pat would lead the others upstairs, where Ann was most likely be held. He knew, from experience, that there were only three possible rooms she could be held in, so they would be split into partners. He and Pat would be together, of course.

"This girl really that important to you?" Dove, the only other female gang member asked as they waited for the all-clear from Bardy. "I wouldn't even go that far for a piece of ass."

"She ain't a piece of ass, Dove," Joe snapped. "She's an innocent. And the only person who believed me when she didn't have to. We don't let people like that die on our watch, alright?"

"Okay, okay," Dove muttered. "Damn."

"Clear!" Bardy called out to Joe and he lead them out from the gathering of bushes they'd been hiding in, each pulling out their weapons as they approached the house. Joe took the safety off his Glock as he immediately started up the stairs. Pat was on his heel. At the top of the stairs, they split into their groups. Dove went with Stu, and Bardy would search another room with TJ, while Pat and Joe took the last room.

"You ready for this?" Pat asked him. "You might not like what you see. She might already be dead."

"I'll hate myself if I don't make sure," Joe responded. "So, yes. I'm ready."

"Fingers crossed." Pat kicked in the door, her gun pointed inside.

The room was completely empty, but for a few chairs and boxes, and three people. The first was the man himself; Sabretooth was a slimy man with a shark's tooth necklace around his neck. He was skinny and tall and his breath constantly stank of onions. It was no wonder he had to stoop as low as rape to get any action. Just the very sight of him made Joe's stomach lurch; he was sickening.

Behind him was a scantily clad, brown-skinned woman with firetruck-red short hair that hung over her eyes in a fringe. She barely even glanced their way, too distracted by the tiny blonde she had her arms wrapped around, her lips attached to the pulse point of a visibly uncomfortable young woman.

Ann. That was Joe's Ann. The same woman who's scrawling cursive he'd read at least twice a week since he was sent away. Her dress was torn and her makeup was smudged and her hair looked like a rat's nest, but there was no mistaking the woman in all the pictures she'd sent him over the years. Only the woman in the pictures was constantly smiling; there was no trace of a smile on her face her. Not even when he could clearly read the look recognition on her face. Instead, he looked absolutely terrified.

"What did you do to her?" Joe barked at Sabe, who just grinned in return.

"Hey to you, too, Joey; how've you been?" he responded. "How was prison?"

"What did you do to her?" Joe repeated, completely ignoring the other man's questions.

"Me?" Sabe asked, as if offended. "Absolutely nothing. My girl, Lourdes, however..."

"GET YOUR HANDS OFF OF HER!" Joe boomed, his gun pointing in the woman's direction. She didn't even blink.

"Don't be ridiculous," Sabretooth laughed. "She knows you won't do anything while she'd wrapped around your girl. Lourdes may be a hoe, but she ain't stupid." He laughed again and pulled his own gun. "I, however, don't care about either bitch." He pointed his gun at them and finally Lourdes stopped, her eyes going wide.

"Sabe?" she asked, stepping away from Ann, who fell to the floor in a fit of sobs. Sabretooth wasted no time in shooting her through the school. Lourdes's body fell to the floor as blood gushed from the wound in her head and Ann screamed. Sabretooth pointed the gun at her next and she began to beg and plead for her life.

"He won't hurt you," Joe told her. "He can't."

"The fuck you mean, I can't?" Sabretooth hissed, his gun trained on Ann's head. "You've seen me shoot bitches before, haven't you? Or have you forgotten?"

"I haven't forgotten what a little bitch you are," Joe said, taking a step forward. Sabe's gun swung around to point at him.

"The fuck you say to me?" he growled. "I ain't no bitch."

Joe scoffed. "Of course you are," he said. "You were my bitch for years and then you left me to be Rick's bitch. And no bitch of Rick's is about to kill his favorite toy; not if he don't wanna be killed in return. Trust me, Sabe, you're a total bitch."

"You wanna see a bitch, motherfucker?" Sabretooth growled. "Why do you watch me waste *yours*?" His head started to swing back but before it could, Ann's hand slapped down on it, forcing the gun out of his grip. It clattered across the floor and she immediately jumped after it. So did Sabretooth, but before he could pull the blonde back, Pat shot his leg and he cried out in pain. "BITCH!" he bellowed.

"You know it," Pat replied, blowing on the muzzle of her gun, before re-holstering it. Ann was able to grab the gun and stood, pointing it down at Sabretooth, who was immobilized by the pain in his leg but looked up at the shaky weapon with defiance.

"What are you gonna do, bitch?" he asked. "Shoot me? You don't got the balls."

Ann glared at him but her hands continued to shake. She took a step back and Sabe laughed. Pat shook her head and glanced up at Joe. "You want me to waste him?" she asked.

"No," Joe said, his eyes trained on Ann. "Let her do it." Ann looked up at that and her eyes pleaded with him. She shook her head. "It's alright," he said. "Think about all the horrible things he did to you. Think about what he did to Lourdes, his own girl. He was about to do the same to you. He deserves this, alright? Nobody would blame you for offin' him. And, trust me, it feels so fuckin' good to do an asshole like that in, to give him what he deserves. Just go ahead and you'll see. Trust me, Ann. Do you trust me?" Ann nodded, but continued to waver. "You'll be okay."

She nodded again and pulled the trigger. The sound the gun made was deafening in the silence of the room. Sabretooth's body went limp after the bullet lodged in his cranium and blood splattered over the floor and Ann's bare feet. The gun dropped from her shaky hand to the ground and her knees began to wobble. She looked to Joe for help and he stepped forward, catching her in his arms before she could reach the floor.

"I've got you," he whispered against her hair. "I've got you, Ann." She buried her face into his chest and began to sob as he rubbed her back.

Pat watched with undisguised hurt, but Joe didn't notice. She took a deep breath and swallowed past the lump in her throat, turning to the other men. "Come on," she said, "we don't wanna be around when the fuzz shows up." She stormed past the confused group, not even sparing Joe and Ann a glance over her shoulder to see that he'd lifted the woman into his arms and was now carrying her, bridal-style, out of the room.

Joe's eyes remained focused on Ann the whole time. "I'm gonna get you outta here, okay?" he whispered in her ear. "You'll be okay. Gonna get you somewhere nice and safe, alright?"

"Okay," Ann sniffed against his shirt, her arms tight around his neck already.

It was in that moment that Ann Martin realized how deeply and fathomlessly in love she was with Joe Sullivan.

Chapter Four

It took them less than 24 hours to get Ann cleaned up, patched up, buy her some new clothes, feed her, and purchase her a train ticket to Stamford, CT. Her family lived in Manhattan, but Joe figured it would be too easy for anybody to snatch her here in the city. At least in Connecticut she would be safe with Pat's cousin, Carly.

"Now, listen," he told her once they made it to Grand Central, "Carly's gonna meet you at the platform. Don't be stupid and go wandering off alone, okay? Somebody might come after you and you don't want to be alone when that happens. Carly's tough and protective as all hell; she's the one that's gonna keep you safe in our absence."

"But, Joe, I—" Ann started to argue.

"No," Joe cut her off, shaking his head. "No arguments right now, okay? We're trying to save your life and this is the best way to do it, okay?" Ann nodded, tears in her eyes. "Okay. Now, as soon as we've got everything settled over here, either me or Pat is gonna come get you in Stamford. We'll call Carly first to let you know we're on our way, okay?" Ann nodded and Joe gave her a gentle smile. "You're gonna be okay, kid," he said, cupping her cheek with one hand. "Everything's gonna be okay now." Ann took a deep breath and canted into him, wrapping her arms around his neck and pressing her face into his neck.

"Don't die," she whispered, on a shuddery breath. She pulled back. "Promise me you won't die." Her gaze was steely and Joe couldn't help but nod at that.

"I promise," he said and she smiled sadly up at him, leaning up on her toes to press her lips against his. Joe returned her kiss, his hands cupping her slender hips. Pat watched from the side with a frown, before looking away.

"Better wrap it up," she said, suddenly, looking at her watch. "The train is leaving in about ten minutes." Joe and Ann pulled apart, sighing. Tears streamed down Ann's cheeks and Joe brushed them away with his thumbs.

"Everything will be alright," he said again. "You'll see. Now, go." He backed away from her and Ann took a deep breath, grabbing her bag and heading in the direction of her platform. Before she reached it, she looked back and locked eyes with Joe. She gave him one last wave and blew him a kiss and he offered her a weak smile in return.

When she was gone, Joe's smile disappeared and he turned to Pat. "Let's go get this asshole," he practically growled, starting towards the exit. Pat was right on his heels.

Infiltrating Rick's brownstone was a much harder feet than they'd originally thought. He lived on a more populated street, so the outdoor guards were not an option. That was good in some ways, Joe thought, but now they had no idea exactly how many people were actually *inside* the damn building because every single window was blocked by thick curtains. And in the daytime, there would be no lights on to give even a shadow so they were going in completely blind.

"Listen," Joe said as they planned it all out. "We may lose a few good men today. But I want you all to know how glad I am to have you all on my side. You've remained loyal to me for all these years and I'm grateful for that. Each one of you has a place in my heart."

"Did prison turn you into a sap, Sullivan?" Bardy growled out, making the others laugh. "'Cause I thought it was supposed to make you tougher."

"Looks like it had the opposite effect," TJ piped in, making them all laugh again.

"Fuck you all," Joe laughed, shaking his head. "Alright," he said, "let's get on with it. If anybody finds that bastard before me, keep him alive; I wanna be the one to put that bullet through his skull, got it?" They nodded and broke apart.

Trying to appear inconspicuous, they split into groups, their weapons concealed by clothing and bags. Dove and Pat linked arms like girlfriends and pretended to gossip about their boyfriends, strutting down the street in tight dresses and heels. One group of their men pretended to whistle at them as they passed; another group was dressed as businessmen and carried their weapons in briefcases. Joe had on a hoodie and a pair of headphones in his ears that weren't actually connected to anything. Nobody noticed that they were headed in the exact same direction.

There was an alley in between Rick's brownstone and the one next to it, which they all slipped into, one group at a time. From there, Joe was able to get a good look at the back of the building, through the slats of a broken fence. "There's a fire escape leading into the yard," he told Pat. "We could probably climb it while the others start from the first floor; corner him, ya know?"

Pat nodded. "Good plan," she said. "But there's one leading out the front, too."

"You take one," Joe said, "I'll take the other." It wasn't too complicated.

"What if he's not alone?"

Joe groaned. "TJ, go with Pat; Bardy, come with me." The men nodded. "All the rest, start from the bottom and make your way up. From the looks of it, we've got three floors to deal with here. Make sure Rick gets to the third floor and, remember, don't kill the bastard. I'll handle that part."

There were murmurs of agreement as everybody got into position. Pat and TJ went around the front and climbed up the fire escape, careful not to pass clear in front of a window, lest they give themselves away. Nobody from the street even glanced their way.

Joe and Bardy situated themselves on the back fire escape while the rest of their team waited at every possible entrance for a sign from them to begin.

"Everybody in position?" Joe whispered in his walkie talkie. There was a static of yeses coming from each individual talkie and he took a deep breath. "Okay. Go!" The sound of windows breaking, doors slamming open, shouts and growls and gunfire coming from inside. Joe and Bardy waited for the signal from Dove, telling them that it was safe to enter.

Ann Martin didn't get on the train. She couldn't. Not when she knew that Joe's life was in danger; not when she just recently realized how she felt about him. She just couldn't do it.

So she stood on the platform for fifteen minutes, waved stupidly to the train as it pulled out of the station, and then walked off the platform. She was almost relieved to see that Joe and Pat were no longer standing in the middle of Grand Central when she arrived, surrounded by a thousand other people desperately trying to find their own platforms. Tourists took pictures of the big clock and the constellations painted on the ceilings. They took in everything with wide eyes and even wider mouths, like this train station was something exceedingly special.

Ann had lived here for the whole of her life and she knew that there was absolutely nothing special about this place once you've seen for the hundredth time. Her parents had taken her through here so many times on their way to and from Westchester County, where they had an estate in Purchase, that it wore off by the time she was five. The train station, which had once been a colorful world full of excitement and adventure for a toddler, was now just...loud.

Ann hastened towards the exit as quickly as possible and breathed in the stale New York City air with reverence. She'd almost died just one day before and she never felt so grateful for the chance to breath in the smoky, polluted air of the city, to hear the thundering stutters of construction just down the street. To experience the hateful scowl on a native's face as they bumped into her on the sidewalk. She felt as if she were experiencing New York for the very first time.

Dragging her rolling suitcase behind her, she started in the direction of Washington Square Park. It would take her a while to get there, she knew that, but maybe she could...

Ann paused. What could she do? She didn't have any guns and she knew nothing she could say to Joe would help. He was intent on his revenge, intent on killing another man no matter what the consequences, and she knew that. Knew that he wouldn't stop until he achieved his goal. He would gladly go back to prison if it meant Rick Silas was dead on the ground.

But Ann couldn't let that happen. She couldn't lose him again, not like this. And any other way than Joe killing Rick meant that Rick killed Joe and she couldn't live with that knowledge either. So, no matter how long the distance, or how high the stakes, Ann would have to go after her love. She had to stop him, even if she risked her own life in the process.

He was completely worth it. At least in her mind. She just hoped that she wasn't too late.

"We lost Paulie!" Fisher's voice crackled through the walkie. Joe cursed and shared a look with Bardy, who'd practically been Paulie's guardian since the day he joined, a gangly kid of about 15, desperate to prove himself. Bardy had made him the weapons master he was now. Or had been.

"Sorry, man," Joe whispered. Bardy shook his head, his eyes filled with undisguised rage.

"He's gonna fuckin' pay for that," he growled in a low voice. Joe nodded, solemnly. His walkie crackled again.

"WE'VE GOT HIM!" Mart shouted through the line. "He's headed toward the third floor. Patti! Joey! Do you read me?!"

"Got it!" Pat's voice called and Joe could hear her without the damn talkie. "I'm goin' in!"

"Me too," Joe growled into the machine as he and Bardy readied their guns and stepped up to the window. "

"You ready for this?" Bardy asked in his low, rumbling voice.

Joe nodded. "As I'll ever be," he replied, taking a deep breath. Bardy nodded in return and they both turned to face the window. Joe held up one hand and started a slow countdown on it.

Three....two.....one!

They burst through the window, spilling glass into the room with them. They stumbled slightly at their entrance, but then held their guns up high, pointing them around the room.

It was small and crowded with bedroom furniture; a bed, a chest of drawers, an old vanity table and matching wooden bookcase. The window was next to the door and in the next second a familiar face appeared in the doorway, his hands held up over his head, a smug smile on his face.

"Rick Silas," Joe growled, then spit at the man's feet as they walked past. "Long time, no see."

Rick's head turned in their direction, hands staying up as Pat entered the room after him, her gun pointed at Rick's head. He smirked at the sight of his old foe. "Joseph Sullivan," he greeted. "I thought you were locked up."

"Got out early," Joe replied, his teeth gritted. "Good behavior and all that."

Rick snorted. "Good behavior? You?" He laughed a big, honking laugh. "Right. Ain't nobody gonna get out of jail for 'good behavior' when a senator's daughter gets off; least of all, you." He shook his head. "So how's you get out then?"

"Not really important," Joe replied, his gun still raised. "I'm out now, ain't I? Why dwell on the past?"

"Joey Sullivan," Rick sighed, "always thinking of the future; almost as much as you think of yourself, you greedy bastard."

"At least I'm not some whiny little bitch," Joe said. "So focused on getting my revenge that I put the lives of others at risk."

"That isn't what you're doing right now?" Rick retorted, his eyes skating over the injured men and women behind Joe's back.

"These are all *willing* participants," Joe informed him. "I didn't kill an innocent just to make a point. I'm no pussy when it comes to revenge, Silas. Not like you."

"Nobody's innocent," Rick said, smartly, his hands finally lowering. "You taught me that." He reached for his pocket and they all took a step forward. He put one hand back up. "Relax," he said, pulling out a butane lighter. He flicked it open, then closed. "Nervous habit," he explained, calmly, that smirk never leaving his face. Joe watched him calculatingly, before his eyes began to roam around the room.

For the first time since they burst in, he realized why there had been such opaque curtains hanging in every single window. On every surface, including the floor itself, there were candles; most lit, but some blown out, though wisps of smoke still rose from their wicks as if they'd been lit recently. It was no surprise, really, considering that Rick was a pyromaniac. He always had a lighter handy and enjoyed watching the wax melt on his candles. His weapon of choice was an impromptu flamethrower made from a can of hairspray and whatever lighter he typically had handy at the given moment.

His favorite had a picture of the Tasmanian Devil on it. More than once, Joe had joked that Taz was like the animated incarnation of Rick himself; crazy and unpredictable and incredibly volatile. Rick apparently still favored the character as Joe could just make out the little brown blob on the otherwise silver piece of metal. Some things never changed, he thought, as he continued to glare at the other man.

"I can't believe you still have that damn thing," Joe said, surprising himself even. He hadn't meant to start a conversation.

"My loyalty to Taz hasn't changed," Rick replied, still flicking the lid of his lighter open and close.

"At least you remained loyal to him," Joe retorted on a growl. "At least you remained loyal to *somebody*."

"Still sore about that, are you?" Rick asked, grinning. "I wish you'd just let it go, man. We weren't *that* close."

"I couldn't give a shit less about your little betrayal," Joe informed him. "But what you did *after* that; killing that girl, sending me to prison to *rot* for five fucking years...you had it coming."

"Had what coming?" Rick asked, still smiling as if he didn't know. Joe cocked his gun in response and Rick's grin widened. "Oh," he said. "That." He took a calm breath and shook his head. "You're not *really* going to kill your best chance at going free, are you?" He flicked the lighter open. "The only person who can confirm that you didn't kill that poor Grant girl." He flicked it closed. "Think about it, Joey; if I'm gone, you're just going to go back to prison." Open.

"Not necessarily," Joe countered.

"What else then? You gonna go on the run?" He tilted his head, his eyes shining with amusement. "With your girl, Pat?" Joe's gun wavered and his mouth tightened. "No..." Rick continued with a titter. "That Martin girl? What's her name?" Joe refused to answer but his hand tightened around the gun. "Ann, right?" Joe still did not respond; he didn't have to. "Ann," Rick decided. "How is she? Still smarting from making her first kill?" Joe's eyes widened.

"How did you know about that?" he barked. Rick didn't even blink.

"You still think I don't have eyes everywhere, don't you?" Rick tutted. "Joey, Joey, Joey...when are you gonna learn? I see *everything*," he whispered, his grin becoming catlike.

"See this, punk!" Pat cried as she took a shot. Joe, at the last minute, shoved her arm, causing her bullet to fly at the hand holding Rick's lighter, which dropped on impulse as the man cursed.

"Fucking bitch!" he screamed as he held his hand to his chest. It was bleeding profusely. Joe glared at Pat.

"What did I fucking say?" he growled. She had the decency to look ashamed.

"Sorry," she grumbled. When he turned back to Rick, he was still holding his bleeding hand. And still cursing. "But he deserved it."

"That don't fucking matter," Joe growled at her. "You don't fucking dis—"

"FIRE!" Bardy screamed from behind them. Pat and Joe looked in the direction he was pointing and did, in fact, see a fire begin to bloom from the curtain, where Rick's lit lighter had fallen.

"Shit!" Joe barked, alerting Rick, who turned and let out a string of curses, starting in the direction of the door. Nearly a dozen weapons rose automatically, pointed straight at his head. He paused, turned and ran for the window—the one without the fire escape. He threw aside the curtain and jumped out while everybody watched in shock.

"Did he just fuckin'—" Pat asked.

"Yes," Bardy growled. "Yes, he did."

Joe wasn't convinced. He ran to the window, even as the flames grew around him.

"Joey!" Pat cried. "What the fuck are you doing? We gotta get outta this fuckin' place before it burns to the ground!"

"Go on!" Joe yelled back. "I need to make sure this sonofabitch is dead! I'll take the fire escape."

The others began to run out, some taking the fire escape while other hightailed it down the stairs. "I ain't leavin' you!" Pat cried, even as Dove started to pull her out. Bardy was urging her towards the fire escape, but she wouldn't go.

Joe ignored her, looking out the window. A sadistic grin spread over his features as he spotted Rick's crumpled body in the grass, joints bent at odd angles. He winced once in sympathy and shook his head, backing away from the window.

The room was now engulfed in flames. Those who had rushed to escape had inadvertently knocked over several candles, which only added to the overall fire. The breathable air was diminishing. Pat still stood at the window, hesitant to leave without him. Bardy was tugging on her arm, trying to get her to leave. She refused, pleading with Joe.

He nodded and started after her, before doubling back. He found the lighter next to the lit up curtains and grabbed it: his trophy. He closed it and tucked it deep into his pocket, before turning on his heel and running towards the fire escape.

He'd barely made it with the curtains of those windows burst into flames too, forcing him back. Pat jumped back as well and Bardy attempted to pick her up, but she struggled too much for him to get a good grip.

"We have to go!" he yelled.

"No!" Pat fought. "I won't leave without him!"

"Pat, go!" Joe ordered. "Get out of here!"

"No!" Pat screamed. "Not until I know you're safe!"

"I've got a plan," Joe called back, before turning and running straight to the other window. He took a deep breath before he took a flying leap straight out of it.

"JOE!" Pat screamed just as Bardy got a good hold of her and carried her down the steps.

Joe had jumped out of windows before, but never on the third floor—not when there wasn't a pool below or something else to break his fall. He'd read somewhere that you could lessen the impact by rolling in midair. Well, whoever said that was apparently an idiot who'd never jumped out of a window in their life.

He rolled as soon as he felt himself fly the air—a front flip that would make any amateur gymnast proud—but it did nothing to numb the impact of the ground as he hit it. If anything, it made the fall worse, more painful. Joe could hear the sickening sound of the bones in his legs cracking as he reached the ground. His spine tingled as if pins and needles were stuck all along it, and the pain as his head connected with the ground was like nothing he'd ever felt before. He saw stars appear in front of his eyes. The entire world went silent for a long moment and he thought he died.

He closed his eyes, welcoming it. He'd done what he'd come here to accomplish. The result was lying about a foot away, in worse shape than him, no doubt. He attempted to turn his head but everything hurt and even with his eyes closed he felt his world spinning on its access. So he just lay there, waiting for death to claim him.

As he waited, a ringing started in his ears, muffled crying rising over it. He started to slowly come back to the world, his eyes creaking open, the world blurried until he blinked a couple times and then...

"Ann?" Joe croaked. "Ann, what—?"

"No," Ann whimpered, placing a finger over his lips. "Don't speak, Joe. You're going to be alright, okay? There's an ambulance on the way; they said not to move you." Joe tried to not but that caused even more pain so he settled for breathing. Ann sniffled. "Oh Joe," she sighed. "Joe, you can't leave me. Not now. I need you, baby. You need to hold out; just a little longer."

"Can't," Joe croaked. "Dying."

"No!" Ann cried. "No, you're not; don't say that."

"But, I-I am," he replied. "And th-that's okay."

"No, it's not!" Ann sobbed. "Don't say that! Please don't say that!" Joe shut his eyes and took a breath. When he opened them again, Pat was there. He turned to look at her.

"Pat," he sighed. "Take...take care of her for me, will ya?"

"Don't talk like that, Joey," Pat sniffled. "You're gonna be just fine, alright? Just fine."

"No," Joe sighed. "I'm not. And if...when I'm not here to protect her...you've gotta...okay? Promise me."

"Joe, I—"

"*Promise*," Joe growled.

Pat took a shuddering breath. "Okay," she said. "I promise."

"Good," Joe breathed, turning his eyes back to Ann.

"She'll take good care of you, okay?" he said. Ann nodded, tearfully.

"So will you," she insisted. "You promised. You promised everything would be alright."

Joe sighed. "I'm sorry," he said. "I don't think I'm...I'm going to be able to..." he trailed off and took another breath. "I'm sorry," he said, closing his eyes. After a long, tense moment, they opened again. "Ann," he breathed. "I...I have to tell you something."

"What?" Ann asked, leaning down again. His voice was becoming faint.

"I...I loved you," Joe breathed out, before his eyes shut permanently and his body went completely limp.

Both Pat and Ann dissolved into tears, the former holding the latter as Ann held on to Joe's body, their tears mingling as they fell to his chest. Above their wails, ambulance sirens could be heard.

THE END

The SCENE OF THE CRIME

27

Aimee Harris

A little exercise wouldn't kill me, she said!

Peggy gasped as she tried to ignore the burning in her legs. When she let Lillian talk her into an early morning jog, she never thought she would need to run for her life in the process!

It was Lillian's fault they were in this mess. She insisted that they leave their cells at home. It would be good for them to 'unplug' for a while. They didn't need constant contact with the world while doing their early morning run. Time to have some quiet time and cleanse the spirit!

Lillian slowed and looked out behind them at the misty wooded path. "I think we lost her."

They both gasped and panted as they kept a sharp eye on the direction they came from. Peggy glared over at her, "Don't say that! That's when the crazy psychotic person jumps out of the shadows."

"We're not in a horror movie." Lillian stated as she straightened up and took in several deep breaths.

"Says the person being chased by Martha-freaking-Stewart with a gun!"

"We don't know if she chased us!" Lillian stated, though her eyes kept focused on the path they just ran. "Maybe she ran when she saw us there. It's not like we waited around to see."

"Ya *think*?" Peggy snapped as she tried to uncurl from around her screaming side. "She just shot someone. What were we going to do? Introduce ourselves? Call 911? Oh wait. We can't do that. We're *unplugging*!"

"Stop." Lillian shushed her, "We're not going to get anywhere with that."

Peggy suppressed an urge to lash out at Lillian as she crouched and tried to regain her composure. It was just supposed to be a quiet run. She just wanted to do the whole 'get active' thing. Forget the rotten week. Get some fresh air. Fresh start on life.

They had started the day long before the sun came up. They had protein shakes, and Lillian drove them out to one of her favorite trails. She had gone on and on about the sunrise the whole time. That and the fact that no one ran these trails at this hour. They would have the woods all to themselves.

And there they were, man and woman having a lovely walk around a clearing. All dressed up They looked like a nice couple, holding hands and talking about who knew what. She remembered Lillian saying something about wanting to find a relationship like that one day.

Then the woman reached into her purse, pulled out a pistol, and shot him. He didn't even know it had happened. He looked so perplexed as he fell sideways onto the ground.

Then the woman turned and saw them. Or Peggy assumed she saw them. One of them might have screamed. Peggy might have screamed. But she could not remember. Everything was a blur after that shot.

"We just need to get to the car." Lillian's tone was matter of fact as she started to retrace her way down the path. "We'll just drive, call 911, and let the police handle everything. We'll be fine."

Peggy clung to Lillian's confidence like a security blanket. That's right. They were set to run. The woman was wearing slacks and a business shirt. What were the chances that she had running shoes on? As long as they kept running, they should be able to make it to the car before the woman had a chance to catch up.

"Right," Peggy said as she hurried to Lillian's side, walking briskly as she ignored the burn in her tired muscles. Even if the woman saw them, they just had to stay way ahead. "But what do we do if she does catch up?"

"She won't catch up."

"But if she *does*?" Peggy insisted.

"Then we deal with it then." Lillian groused impatiently.

Peggy felt a new wave of anxiety as she took a mental inventory of what they had. No electronics. Cells, iPod, and every other piece of modern civilization was left behind in the car. No back packs. No pepper spray. They just had the running suits on their backs, some water, and trail mix. It was supposed to be *good* to get away from the world for a few hours!

"Deal with it. Right. You subdue her with your shoelaces, and I will hydrate her to death." Peggy glanced over her shoulder nervously. Even if she was confident they could handle getting to the car, she couldn't outrun a bullet. If anything happened, she hoped that the woman had terrible aim. Worse eyesight. And cataracts. Cataracts would be most appreciated. Maybe a real bad hip...

Lillian didn't bother to respond. This scared Peggy more than anything. It never mattered what kind of a jam they got into, Lil always had an answer for everything. A witty retort. A clever solution. *Something*!

Before she could push for a further reply, she heard the faint sound of an engine in the distance. She let out a sigh of relief. Safe! Someone was in the area, and they likely at a phone. At the very least they could get her and Lillian back to their car. Or better yet, to town.

"Lil, do you hear it?" Peggy asked insistently. Peggy squinted through the morning fog, trying to see where the sound was coming from. She didn't see any headlights in the distance. In the quiet of the morning it was hard to tell exactly where the vehicle was.

"Peg.." Lillian grabbed her by the elbow and started pulling her toward the side of the road. "Get out of sight."

Peggy opened her mouth to protest. They didn't need to get out of sight. They needed to hurry and get some assistance! She froze when she saw Lillian looking back from where they came, nearly getting pulled off her feet as Lillian all but dragged her to the brush covered edge of the road. A pair of headlights were making their way closer through the fog.

Peggy's heart jumped into her throat as she scrambled to keep up with Lillian. She crouched low as a small ATV made its way down the path. The woman looked out of place as she cruised and studied the area. She looked very calm and dainty atop the machine. She would probably reach Peggy's shoulders if they stood beside each other. Not that Peggy was ever inviting the opportunity. The woman wore a laced business blouse with a high collar. She wore the blood on her face and shirt like a new fashion statement. She did not seem to mind the fact she was splattered with someone's blood in the least.

Peggy held her breath as the woman came close. She and Lillian huddled shoulder to shoulder as they watched her slowly pass by. Peggy's mind whirled. What if she found the car? Would she notice? Would she just wait there for them? What if she had seen them at the scene after all?

The sound of the motor was deafening. Peggy did not even dare to blink. Sweat poured down her spine as she waited for the woman to make her way past.

She started to let out a slow breath as the woman passed. She and Lillian could find a way back. Even if they didn't chance the car, they could eventually walk to civilization. They just had to keep their heads on straight. Everything would be okay. Then they could call the police. They'd find the crime scene and take care of everything. Surely that place was littered with evidence and stuff.

The ATV sputtered as the woman coasted to a stop, and to Peggy's horror she backed slowly up as her eyes trained on their hiding spot. She gave a warm, charming smile as she tilted her head speculatively to the side.

Peggy felt cold as the woman stared in their direction. A seed of terror grew in her chest at the woman's calm and welcoming demeanor. Welcoming, with dark intent rippling under the surface. A spider beckoning flies into her presence. She flinched as the woman pulled a leg over the edge of the machine to dismount.

Panic blinded Peggy as she saw the woman lift her delicate hand, a pistol flashing faintly in the morning light. She didn't know if she made a sound. She didn't know if there was a sign or anything to run. She didn't even realize she had started running until she felt a branch slap into her face as she crashed through the brush.

She caught a flash of light out of the corner of her eye and she glanced over in terror. To her mixed relief and horror she saw the neon reflective safety tape on Lillian's running shirt. It flashed in the morning light with each step, made all the more obvious by the shadows.

There was a sharp cracking sound and Lillian crashed to the ground. Peggy stumbled behind a tree for cover. The pounding of her heart in her ears deafened out the sounds around her. She saw Peggy holding her hip and trying to keep low to the ground. But she couldn't hear her. She struggled to take a breath as her throat constricted. The woman picked her way toward them, the kindly smile replaced with cold, calculating determination.

Peggy suppressed a sob as she looked around frantically. The branches that lay on the ground were dry and brittle. There was nothing that looked like it would be any defense against a woman with a pistol. She crouched behind her partial shield as she tried to keep an eye on the woman and Lillian.

As the woman approached, Peggy leaped from her hiding place. The woman took a step back, startled at the sudden attack. Peggy didn't know which of them was more surprised. She clutched frantically at the weapon. She felt the stab of long nails dig into the flesh of her hand as the woman tried to dislodge her. They grappled frantically for the weapon.

As they crashed to the ground, Peggy heard Lillian's shrill voice. She couldn't make out the words as she wrenched the weapon away, flinching and trying to guard her face from grasping and clawing fingers.

She clutched the weapon in both hands as she pointed it at her attacker. The woman backed away with hands up. Peggy's first instinct was to fire the weapon. Restraining herself felt almost as painful as the welting scratches burning on her arms and face. She and the woman sized each other up as Lillian made her way awkwardly onto her feet. Blood soaked her pants leg as she limped forward.

"Why?" Peggy demanded of the woman, who did not respond as she slowly circled to one side with hands up in surrender. A slight shrug. An almost dismissive gesture. Peggy felt rage mix in with the fear. How could anyone be so calm about this? The woman couldn't possibly feel nothing about killing a man and running down two accidental onlookers? There was no way she could possibly be as calm as she looked. She practically looked like she was about to host a blood spattered Tupperware party!

"Why??" Peggy practically shrieked as she held the weapon on the woman. The silence was probably worse than anything the woman could have said. The unspoken reason for this casual killing spree. The woman slowly reached up and fixed a wayward piece of graying hair at her temple.

"Let's go Peg." Lillian said frantically, skin sheet white. Her voice was hoarse as she clutched at her leg in with a grimace. Peggy wanted to say no. She wanted to get answers. She wanted to keep the psychopath in her sight. The urge to shoot the woman was overwhelming.

"Peg!" Lillian's voice cut through the haze of confusion that suffocated her. A wave of shame edges into the rage. She couldn't pull the trigger. She tried to will it of herself. But she couldn't. They needed to get to a phone. They needed to call the police. And they needed to be safe. They need to turn this freaking psychopath into the police and get her off the streets!

"Lil, go call the police." Peggy kept wary attention on the woman as she started waving her companion toward the road.

"You've got to be kidding me!"

"Go call the police and get to a hospital!" Peg said as she tried to control the trembling that was seeping into her muscles. "Just hurry up and use her ride, okay?"

"You're not going to—?"

"No!" she started, "Not unless she gives me a reason."

The second half was more for the benefit of the psycho woman. She didn't *want* to be left alone with the monster. But what else could be done? They could not just leave a killer out here to disappear. They couldn't put all three on the ATV, and Lillian was bleeding badly. She couldn't walk the mile or so back to the car. They had to separate.

Lillian gave the woman a murderous glare. If their roles were reversed, she had a feeling Lillian would not have paused on the trigger. Peggy didn't even know if she was doing the right thing herself. How do you validate letting someone live when they have no value for life?

If the woman felt one way or the other about the outcome, she did not show it. She did not even seem particularly upset about the fact they were about to turn her in. Peggy could not shake the chill the woman brought on. Lillian did not seem happy with the turn of events either. She looked between the two uncertainly. This was a first. It was always Lillian with all the answers. But then again this was a far cry from work troubles or a troublesome clingy ex.

"It's okay. Go get your leg checked out." Peggy insisted as she kept the weapon trained on the woman. "Send the cops. It'll be okay."

She felt herself regretting her decision a moment later when Lillian managed to awkwardly limp to the ATV and race off on it. She was relieved at the same time. Lillian would find the car and help would be on the way.

The day was starting to brighten as she started herding the woman toward the trail. Her heart raced as she kept an eye out for any signs of another attack. But the woman was oddly accommodating as they picked their way out of the brush and started their way down the road.

"I suppose I should thank you."

Peggy nearly jumped out of her skin at the voice. The woman's voice was so calm as she walked along with her hands still raised and in sight. Her voice was almost pleasant. Though it was prickling, oily kind of kindness. Laced in venom.

"Why?" Peggy found herself asking again.

"For making things so much easier." the woman said with an almost wistful sigh. "Everything always seems to work out in the end, no? My poor husband. He was such a dedicated pillar of the community. A sweet man when it came down to it. Brings me here every week just to get away from the world a little while. Just the two of us. Politics would have ruined us though. There were too many skeletons in our closets that didn't need aired to our acquaintances."

"So you killed him?"

The woman didn't answer, though she did manage a muffled sniff as they walked along. She tried to make sense of it. "Why are you thanking me?"

"You made things so much simpler, dear." the woman said in an eerily kind voice. As she spoke she took in several quick breaths crumbled in on herself, suddenly looking very frail and vulnerable. So tiny and practically helpless in her situation.

"Like it's going to fool anyone!" Peggy thought angrily. The woman's real nature was burned so far into her memory that she would have nightmares. This was far from the quiet morning run she and Lillian had planned. The opposite of in fact.

Before Peggy could react, she noticed the flash of lights racing down the narrow path. Her heart leapt in joy as she realized it was the police. That was fast! Did Lillian even have time to get to the car yet? Maybe a hiker heard the shot and called it in. It didn't matter. They were here! The nightmare was almost over.

She smiled in relief as the policemen jumped out of the car, guns drawn..

They were pointing their weapons at her! Peggy froze in confusion as the men started to scream at her to put down her weapon. They must not have talked to Lillian.. Oh no. Probably not. They came way too fast to have stopped to ask any questions. She carefully moved as she dropped the weapon, trying not to agitate the situation.

"You killed my husband!" the woman wailed as she backed away from Peggy. Crocodile tears streamed down her face as she seemed to try to shield herself.

Peggy stared incredulously as the woman was grabbed and pulled away. She opened her mouth to warn them, but the next thing she knew she was face first in the dirt. She gasped as she heard voices yelling at her to stay down. To not move.

"It was her!" She gasped as she tried to turn, only to be manhandled flat onto the ground.

"Are you alright, Mrs. Jameson?" One of the police asked the psychotic woman as she made a show of grief and shock. "It's alright. We got your call. Both the attackers are in custody. Can we ask you a few questions? Can you tell us where your husband is?"

Peggy blinked. Attackers? Two? Where was Lillian? What was happening?

I really must thank you.

No!

"It was her!" Peggy said again. But no one was listening as she was hefted to her feet. The lights were blinding as she was surrounded by a blur of voices and lights. The pleasant quiet of the morning shattered.

THE DEER WOMAN

COURTNEY VAUGHN

The grass on the prairie swayed in the wind as the guineas clucked and plucked ticks from the dry, cracked earth. Pigs snorted into their slop trough and squealed as they rooted one another aside, trying to fill their bellies. Their ears twitched as the flies tried to rest on them. The tiny black wings and feet tickled wherever they landed. Beads of perspiration caught in Sarah's eyelashes and stung her eyes. She wiped her forehead with her arm. Dust turned to mud in the streams of her sweat.

She picked up the bucket that she had balanced on the knotty fence. The smell of the pigs was as familiar to her as the wrinkles on her calloused hands. In the distance, thunder faintly rumbled. Sarah shielded her eyes with her hand and peered into the distance. Hopefully the rain would make it to them this time. The crops were parched, and the well was low. The wooden bucket banged against her hip as she lugged it back to the house. The rough, rope handle sawed against her palm.

Jacob's weather-worn boots were on the front porch. They had a hole in the bottom of the soul, but even so they were his better pair of shoes. The wooden slats creaked under her weight as she pulled open the door. It drooped in a lopsided fashion that left a small gap at the top even when it was closed. The bottom corner had grated against the porch until an arc was scarred into the slats, marking its path. Sarah's eyes took a moment to adjust to the dimness of their little home.

In the far right corner she could make out their bed. It was draped with a threadbare, patchwork quilt that Jacob's mother had given them as a wedding present ten years ago. The other side of the house had a wobbly table Jacob had handcrafted for them. His hands were better suited to praying than they were to manual labor. Three stools sat beside the table. Two of them were well worn and smooth from years of sitting. The third one was just as rough as the day it was made. Jacob had made it for their future child, but they had not been blessed with that yet. Looking at the stool made Sarah ache inside, but putting it away would feel like giving up.

Sarah placed the bucket by the fireplace. The hearth was made from river stones that the Heely boys had dug out for them in exchange for helping their ma through childbirth. Money was sparse, so people did what they could for one another. Mostly manual labor or a few ears of corn were used for payment of services. Sarah ran the edge of her hand across the table to scrape away crumbs from breakfast. She caught them in her other hand and dusted them into the slop bucket. Her white apron was tinged brown with sweat stains and dirt. She lifted the hem to wipe off her face as she heard hooves clopping against the ground outside. She straightened her apron and headed back out into the sun's heat.

The Doc was waiting for her in the yard as the wooden door fell shut against the door frame behind her. "Hello, Mrs. Cartwright. You ready?" A gray mare was following behind the buckskin he was riding.

"Afternoon, Doc." She took the reins to the mare from his outstretched hand and placed her left foot in the stirrup before swinging herself up into the saddle. "Alright, let's go." Sarah patted the side of Maggie's neck as she urged the horse to follow Doc further into the prairie. Her gait was steady as they plodded across the ground.

Sarah helped Doc Brannigan from time to time with births and minor wounds. When the town was as small as Fort Marshall, people had to lend a hand when they could just to make due. Today she and Doc were heading over to the Indian camp just past Hindman's Ridge. The Kiowa allowed Doc and herself to barter for medicinal herbs. Doc had helped the chief's daughter when she was attacked by a bear. He had found her bleeding on the plains and had patched her up. The braves found him tending to her and brought them both back to the tribe. When the girl had survived her wounds, Chief Two Crows had allowed Doc to live, and as part of his appreciation offered access to their medicines.

Buzzards circled off to the right as they rode. Another wave of thunder rumbled in the distance. Maggie's ears twitched as she listened to the thunder roll over the sounds of the crickets in the grass. A breeze bowed the tall grass of the plains and played with flyaway hairs that framed Sarah's face. Doc straightened himself in his saddle. Riding was becoming more of an issue for him as he got older.

"Doing ok, Doc?"

"It's just the weather. Wreaks havoc on my joints." His graying hair feathered around his head in the wind.

"Do we need to take a break?" Sarah's worry lines furrowed as she looked at him.

Doc shook his head and smiled through the pain, "No, we need to get this done before the storm hits." He always put the wellbeing of others before his own. The Reagan baby had a case of cholera. The Kiowa had chokecherry bark and few other things Doc needed.

It was about an hour before the tribe came into view. Sarah could see the smoke from their fires before she could see the teepees. As they got closer, she could see the people moving about. Half-naked children ran around the camp chasing one another. Braves fashioned arrows and spears. Squaws tended to meat cooking over a fire and shucked corn. A few of the children called out in trilling noises as the two riders approached. Pale Sparrow emerged from a flap in a deerskin teepee and greeted them. She had been found by the Kiowa when she was eight. Her blonde hair was in a plated braid over her shoulder. Her family had been killed in a shootout. She was the only survivor. Pale Sparrow had learned their language and had managed to keep most of her own as well. She served as the translator for their meetings.

Doc eased himself out of his saddle and handed his reins to a young boy who had run up to them eagerly. Doc pulled a bundle out of his saddle bag and secured it under his arm. He tousled the boy's dark hair as he walked past him to Pale Sparrow who greeted them with a smile. Sarah slid off of Maggie and handed her horse's reins to the boy as well.

The horses followed him willingly to a wooden post where he tied them up. She longingly watched the boy and a few other children run off to play while Pale Sparrow and Doc greeted one another.

"Blessings." Pale Sparrow held the doctor's hand in hers and embraced Sarah warmly as she broke out of her trance and joined them.

"Blessings," Doc gestured to the goods under his arm, "I need to see Wandering Coyote."

Pale Sparrow bowed her head and lifted the flap in the teepee she had emerged from earlier. Sarah followed Doc into the hide structure. It smelled like tobacco and nutmeg inside. Wandering Coyote was sitting cross legged in front of a small fire. The warmth was almost sweltering. He wore a bear's claw around his neck on a leather chord. Feathers decorated small braids in his long, dark hair. His skin was wrinkled, and one eye was clouded over. He gestured for them to sit with him.

Doc unrolled the bundle he had carried with him. He had brought some corn whiskey, some metal spoons, and a steel knife. Wandering Coyote picked up each item in his hands and looked them over. He turned his gaze to Pale Sparrow and nodded.

"What do you need today?" Behind her were leather pouches stuffed with dried herbs and bits of roots.

"Chokecherry bark, blackberry root, and wild ginger." Doc wiped sweat away from his eyes while she loaded a pouch with what they needed. She also gave them a few more things that Sarah didn't recognize. Once the pouch was full, Pale Sparrow handed it to Doc. She followed them back outside as they headed for their horses. The blonde woman took Sarah's arm and pulled her aside as Doc tucked the medicine into this saddle bag.

"I saw you looking at the children." Pale Sparrow handed Sarah a small pouch of her own. "This is red clover. Boil the leaves and drink the tea from it. It will help with fertility."

Sarah was taken aback. Her eyes brimmed with tears of gratitude as she closed her hand on the pouch of herbs. She hugged Pale Sparrow tightly and whispered in her ear, "Thank you." She clutched the small leather satchel in her hand as she climbed back on Maggie's bony back.

The wind was picking up now. Doc urged his horse to gallop faster. Maggie lagged behind. Her age made it harder for her to keep up. Her breath felt labored under Sarah's weight. Tiny water droplets splattered on Sarah's hands and trickled through her hair to her scalp. The coldness of the rain awakened goosebumps on her arms.

Jacob was waiting on the porch when they arrived back at the Cartwright's home. He rushed out into the rain to hold Maggie still as his wife climbed out of the saddle. He handed the reins to Doc. The two men tilted their heads to one another, and Doc trotted off in the direction of the rest of the town. Rain started to pelt harder on the ground, turning the parched dirt to mud.

Sarah let out a sigh of relief as she pulled off her wet clothes and laid them in front the fire Jacob had built. She tucked the pouch with the red clover under her wet apron so Jacob wouldn't see it. The burning wood hissed as a few drops of rain found their way down the chimney. "How is Mr. Gains doing?"

"He's near the end." Jacob had sat with the family as they prayed over the old man. There was nothing left that Doc could do for him, so as the town preacher it was time for Jacob to step in. Mr. Gains' time had run its course. "He has maybe a few days left. A week at the most."

Jacob watched his wife as she pulled a night dress on. She was still as beautiful as the day he had married her. Sarah pulled a few potatoes from a sack and started peeling them. Jacob walked up behind her and encircled her waist in his arms. He held her close and swayed back and forth with her.

"You're going to make me cut myself." Sarah laughed as she held the knife in one hand and the potato in the other. She turned her head to kiss her husband. His dark whiskers scratched at her cheek.

"What do you need me to do?" Jacob let her go after the kiss and pushed up his sleeves. He shook his black hair out of his eyes.

"Could you fill the pot with some water and hang it by the fire to boil?" Sarah used the knife in her hand to point to a black pot with a metal handle sitting by the hearth.

Jacob picked up a ladle from their water bucket and dropped a few scoops into the pot before hanging it by the handle on the hook above the fire. He repositioned one of the stools so that he could sit across from her while she cooked. He lifted his worn bible from the corner of the table and picked it up to read to her. "Deuteronomy, chapter thirty-one, verse eight: And the Lord, He is the One who goes before you. He will be with you; He will not leave you nor forsake you; do not fear nor be dismayed."

In all the years of being a preacher's wife, Sarah never got tired of hearing her husband read scriptures to her. His voice was kind and loving. The pages of his bible were thin and faded from years of use. Corners were bent to mark his favorite verses. Her knife chopped rhythmically as he read. She carried the potatoes to the pot and dumped them in. The water was barely starting to bubble. She chopped up a carrot and an onion and added them as well. Flour sprinkled from her hand into the pot as she thickened the soup. A dash of salt and pepper floated on top of the broth as she stirred everything in.

Thunder shook the house. Outside, the pigs squealed in terror as lightening carved its way across the sky. Sarah sipped the broth. It still tasted mostly like water, but it was the best she could do with what they had right now. The next coach with a delivery for the General Store was still a few weeks away, and Mr. and Mrs. Harper were already low on everything.

Once the potatoes and carrots were soft, Sarah ladled some of the soup into a bowl and placed it on the table in front of her husband. He smiled at her gratefully and pulled it closer to him as she filled her own bowl and joined him at the table.

Jacob reached out for Sarah's hands, and they both bowed their heads. Fire light reflected off of their faces as Jacob began saying grace, "Father God, we thank you for this meal we are about to eat and ask that you let it nourish our bodies. We ask that you please be with Mr. Gains and his family and help them through the days to come. We ask that if it is your will, that we be blessed with a child, and that you help us to always follow your path. Thank you for the rain and for Sarah and the Doc's safe journey today. I ask that you speak through me this Sunday as I give my sermon, and in your name we pray, amen."

"Amen," Sarah echoed softly after him. She sipped her soup, but her mind kept wandering to the herbs stashed under her apron. She was worried that if Jacob knew about them he would think she was taking the pregnancy into her own hands and out of God's. Maybe God wanted Pale Sparrow to give her the herbs. Maybe this was His way of helping her when even her own body seemed against her. It was one thing to use herbs as medicine for a cold, but to use them in the hopes of conceiving a child felt almost like witchcraft. Sarah chewed a piece of potato slowly as she thought about the decision she would have to make.

"Are you ok?" Jacob sat down his bowl and touched her hand lightly. "You look worried and far away."

His words brought her out of her thoughts, and she smiled at him reassuringly, "Yes, I'm fine. Just worried about the Doc." Sarah tilted her head down as she looked into her bowl, "His arthritis is getting bad, and this weather always makes it worse."

"Well, we can go look in on him in the morning. Would that make you feel better?" He ran his thumb over the back of her hand.

Sarah wove her fingers between his and nodded, "Yes."

Outside, horses whinnied in distress between thunderclaps, and a loud unnatural crack echoed. Jacob stood up from the table. His stool clattered to the floor behind him as he rushed to the door. Sarah's heartbeat thudded against her ribcage. Her husband's figure was silhouetted in the doorframe as lightening arched across the sky.

"What is it?" Sarah found herself on her feet. Her voice was lost in the next rumble of thunder.

Jacob ran into the yard. The door slammed shut behind him. Sarah's bare feet padded against the floor as she raced to see what was going on. Her hand flung open the door. Through the curtain of rain, she saw Jacob hunched over a heap in their yard. Another flash of lightening revealed a stagecoach that was tilted on its side. One wheel was spinning in the air. Rain bounced off of the body of the wagon and into the already forming puddles. Jacob climbed on top of the wagon and jerked the door open. Sarah saw the top half of his body reach into the coach. She was standing on the porch. A small puddle of water gathered in a dip in the wood. Jacob's head emerged from the wreckage. Something was cradled in his arms.

"Sarah!" He yelled out over the storm.

Sarah's feet splashed across the porch. Cold mud squelched between her toes. She stood on her tiptoes as Jacob leaned over and handed her the bundle in his arms. As her arms cradled it, she could feel the slight movement of tiny hands and feet. It was a baby swaddled in a dark blanket. A cry erupted from the bundle as the child squirmed in her arms. Rain was soaking into the blanket. Sarah looked back up at her husband. He was trying to lift another man out of the coach. Jacob managed to get the man's arm looped over his shoulder as he struggled to get leverage. His boots slid on the wet wood as he tried to brace both himself and the added body weight of the other man. Sarah noticed that the coach's passenger was offering no help at all. His body was completely limp as Jacob fought to get them both back onto the ground safely.

Bracing the child against her chest, Sarah padded back up onto the porch and over to the door. She held it open as her husband towed the stranger across the lawn. The toes of the man's boots drug across the ground, leaving behind a trail in the mud. Jacob laid the man down on the floor in front of the fire. He wadded up Sarah's clothing that she had laid there to dry earlier and tucked them under the man's head as a make shift pillow. Sarah held the whimpering child up to her shoulder and rocked it gently while she watched her husband lower his ear to the man's mouth and then his chest. Jacob couldn't feel any breath coming from the man's nose or mouth, and he couldn't hear any heartbeat.

"Stay here!" Jacob pointed his finger sternly at his wife as he ran back out into the night.

Sarah paced nervously near the bed trying to calm the baby, "Shhh. You're ok. It's ok." Her body bounced lightly with each step. The rhythmic jostling soothed him. "It's ok, little one." Slowly the child's crying stopped. "There. See? You're ok. You're ok, baby."

The door flung open, startling Sarah. Her heart flew into her throat as she looked into the darkness. Doc stepped across the threshold followed by Jacob. Both of them were drenched from the raging storm.

"Over by the fire." Jacob jerked his head towards the man's unconscious body.

Doc knelt by the man's head and kneaded his neck with his fingers trying to find a pulse. The fire flickered and sputtered as the rain continued to find its way down the chimney. Doc shook his head and started doing chest compressions, occasionally pausing to blow into the man's mouth. After a few moments he paused, "He's gone. Most likely killed in the crash." Doc stood up, bracing his back with his hands. The joints in his knees groaned and popped as he stood up. He motioned towards Sarah with his hands, urging her closer, "Let's take a look at the little one."

Sarah carried the baby over to Doc and folded her arms anxiously over her chest, "What'll happen to it now?"

"Well first," Doc laid the baby on the table and unwrapped the blanket, "let's make sure it's healthy."

The baby looked less than a year old. Under the blanket, the child was naked except for a cloth diaper that was pinned on its bottom. It had a tuft of dark hair on its tiny head, and blue eyes looked up at them. Doc unpinned the diaper that was wrapped around it. As the cloth was pulled back, they saw it was a baby boy. He kicked his legs trying to wriggle away. Doc looked him over from head to toe checking for any sign of trauma or bruising.

"He looks healthy enough. No sign of swelling or any bruises." He pinned the diaper back on the baby. Sarah brought him a dry strip of cloth to wrap the child in so the blanket could dry. "In the morning we can send word to a few of the towns nearby to see if anyone knows about a man and a baby on a stagecoach. Any luck, someone will know who they are."

"What about tonight?" Jacob was staring at the man lying in their floor.

"If you can help me get him on my horse, I can take the body to the undertaker's for storage. Maybe drop the baby off with the school teacher?"

Sarah scooped up the baby, "There's no need to bother Miss Adams at this time of night. We can watch over him."

Doc turned to look at Sarah with solemn, understanding eyes, "Well, alright then. I'll drop by in the morning with some milk for him." He nodded to Jacob who grabbed the man's boots as Doc bent down with a groan to grab his shoulders.

The two men hobbled outside with the body, leaving Sarah alone with the baby. "Sweet, sweet baby." She cooed over him and he nestled his head in the curve of her neck. Sarah felt an overwhelming wave of love and appreciation. Her eyes flitted up towards heaven as her lips quivered into a smile. The baby's soft breath pulsed into her throat. A whisper escaped from her, "Thank you." She felt more blessed in that moment than she had in her entire life.

Jacob came back in the house and sloughed off his soaked boots. Tiny clods of mud tumbled off of their soles as he sat them by the door. He slowly approached his wife who was swaying slightly from side to side with the baby cuddled up next to her. He noticed small tears trickling down her cheeks, "Hey, are you ok?" Jacob cupped her face gently in his hands.

Sarah nodded with a small laugh, "Yes, I'm wonderful." Her eyes sparkled in the firelight. "Jake, what if this is God's way of giving us a baby?" Her voice was hesitant as she searched his face for a reaction. She bit her bottom lip as her face beamed with hope and joy.

"Sarah, this child could have a mother out there somewhere who is missing him terribly...we can't keep him." Jacob's eyes were full of sadness as he stroked her cheek with his thumb.

"If we can't find his family, he will need someone to take care of him." Sarah clutched the baby closer to her body, "Why can't that be us?"

Jacob sighed and rubbed his temples. He paced the length of the room as he thought about how to handle the situation. He had wanted a child as badly as his wife had, and they had tried for years. He faced her once more. Her hope was tangible in the air around them. "Ok," Jacob's voice was tentative, "if we make an honest effort to find his family, and no one comes forward, then we can take care of him."

"Ok." Sarah choked back laughter of elated happiness as she hugged her husband and held the baby between them. The two of them looked down at his face. "He'll need a name."

"Try not to get too attached, darling. We don't know how long we'll have him." The joy in Sarah's eyes dimmed as he spoke, "But, I guess we will have to call him something while he's here." Jacob stroked her hair.

"Gabriel." Sarah whispered over the sleeping baby in her arms.

"Gabriel." Jacob echoed as he touched the baby's head gently. He tried to fight back the joy he felt seeing his wife with a baby in her arms.

She would be heartbroken if the baby's family was found. After years of failure to conceive, Jacob didn't know if she could take that kind of heart ache. He silently prayed that the child didn't have anyone else. Part of him felt disgusted at himself for wishing such horrible things, but part of him still hoped it was true.

Sarah pulled a woven basket out of the corner of the room and filled it with scraps of cloth to create a makeshift bed for the child. She set it by the side of their bed and nestled Gabriel inside. Jacob pulled off his wet clothing and clumsily knelt beside the bed. Sarah joined him as he prayed, but she kept one hand on the basket where Gabriel was sleeping as her husband's voice quietly drifted into the night.

"Father God, we ask for your guidance with this child. We ask that if he has family, you let them hear word of his safe rescue. We ask that if he is alone in this world that you give us your blessing on raising him up to be a Godly man. We ask that you look after the soul of the man who lost his life tonight, and that you bring him and his family peace, dear Lord. Thank you for our home and this small blessing that you have brought to us, no matter how long or short that blessing may last. Please keep us on your path and guide us towards your will. In your name we pray, amen."

"Amen." Sarah turned her face towards Gabriel as the prayer finished. In her heart she felt that he was already hers.

Jacob climbed into bed and scooted himself up against the wall to make room for his wife. Sarah laid herself down beside her husband. She let one hand dangle off of the side of the bed to touch the basket. Touching his bed reassured her that it was real and not just a dream. Jacob's arm wrapped around her as they settled in. For once, she felt like her family was complete. After a few hours of gazing lovingly down at Gabriel, Sarah finally drifted off to sleep.

The sound of a rooster broke through Sarah's peaceful dreams. Gabriel whined softly in his basket. Sarah leaned over the edge of the bed and picked him up. "Hi, baby boy. Good morning." Her voice was soothing as she cradled him close to her.

Jacob stirred next to her. He propped himself up on his elbows. A sleepy smile spread across his face. He sat up and kissed Sarah on the shoulder. "Good morning."

"Hi," she whispered back lovingly.

"How is the little man doing?"

"A little fussy. He's probably hungry." Sarah shifted so that Jacob could take Gabriel from her arms.

"Doc should be back by soon." The tiny body felt so fragile in his arms. He leaned in and kissed the baby's forehead before handing him back to Sarah. "I need to get dressed. We have a lot to do today."

Sarah lifted Gabriel's basket and carried it over to the table. She laid him back down while she went about cooking breakfast. She watched Jake pull up his trousers and slip his feet into the boots he wore last night. There was a slight squelching sound as his feet pressed against the soles. His other pair of shoes were most likely still soaked from sitting on the porch all night, so he would have to make due. Sarah made a mental note to set them out in the sun later.

Thick oatmeal fell off of the wooden stirring spoon into a bowl. Sarah dusted the top of the blob with the last of their remaining sugar and passed it to Jacob. She dished herself out a small portion and sat beside the baby at the table. Jacob blew on his food and said a brief prayer to bless their day. As they ate, the sound of boots walking across the porch came through the door followed by a rapping knock.

"Come on in, Doc." Jacob's words were muffled through his food.

Doc Brannigan opened the door, "Good morning. How is my littlest patient, hmm?"

"He'll be a lot better once he's had some of that milk you're carrying." Sarah stood up as Doc handed her a bottle of milk.

"I had a spare in the cupboard. The rubber tip has seen a few teething infants, but it should still do the trick." Doc watched as Sarah picked up the baby and brought the bottle to his lips. "Oh, before I forget, here's some extra milk from the Canady's. Helen says you just come on over if you need anything." He placed a glass jug of milk on the table.

"Thank you, Doc. I'll make sure to stop by later and thank Mrs. Canady. I'm sure she'll want to see where the milk is going." Sarah watched delightedly as Gabriel took to the bottle. His blue eyes stared up at her as he fed.

"I've got Thomas sending out a telegram to Canyon City, and Luke said he had to make a ride out to Darby Ridge today, so he's taking word that way. Undertaker said he can keep the body for a week before the stench gets too bad. Maybe something will turn up." Doc ran his hand over his leathery neck. "Well, Jacob, do you have any plans for that coach outside?"

"Reckon I'll see if we can fix it. Town could use a new stagecoach."

"I think Mr. Havisham would be greatly obliged to that." Doc smiled.

Jacob finished off the rest of his oatmeal and stood up, "Let's go take a look at it." He kissed Sarah and the baby before walking outside with Doc.

Sarah watched as Gabriel's eyes slowly drifted closed. His belly was full, and he was ready to sleep again. She nestled him back into his basket and put on her dirty clothes that had dried by the fire. She would get Jake's clothes from him tonight and wash up some laundry by the creek tomorrow. The red clover fell out of its hiding place as she picked up her apron. Sarah ran her fingers over the soft leather pouch. She turned to face Gabriel. Maybe she wouldn't need the herbs after all. The floor creaked a little as she walked over to the hope chest her mother had given her on her wedding day. A thin layer of dust covered the top of the chest as she lifted the lid and sifted through the lace curtains and copper pots. She buried the small leather pouch at the bottom of the chest and shut the lid.

Outside, she could hear wood creaking and the muffled sound of the men's voices as they looked over the wagon. Sarah tidied up the kitchen and straightened the blanket on the bed. The heat of the day was already starting to seep into the small house. She picked up the basket with Gabriel in it and headed outside to gather eggs before it got much hotter.

The days wore on quickly and happily for Jacob and Sarah. Sarah hadn't stopped smiling since she had taken in Gabriel. The first few weeks were the hardest. She was always worrying if someone would come to claim him, but as time went on that fear steadily diminished. Days turned to weeks, and weeks melted into months. Gabriel was a happy addition to their family, and even though numerous telegrams had been sent, no one had come to collect the baby. The man who had died in the rainy night that Gabe came to live with them was given a nameless grave marked with a wooden cross. The child brought them so much joy, it was hard to imagine their lives without him now. Some of the other women were able to spare a few pieces of clothing that their children had out grown, and other supplies were donated as needed. Jacob had offered to build him a crib, but luckily Mr. Havisham constructed one before he could. It was a thank you gift for the stagecoach he used to transport families and goods between the towns.

The weather was beginning to cool off some. The sweat of summer no longer hung humidly in the air. The pigs were becoming lazy as the days shortened and their bodies grew plumper. Some of them would be slaughtered in a few more months to make a Christmas dinner for the town. Doc's body was becoming less and less cooperative as the colder weather moved in. He was drinking herbal teas from the Kiowa almost daily to fight the pain in his joints. There had been a few times that Sarah had to ride out to the tribe on her own to get his medicine because of how poorly he was doing. Jacob had been furious with her when he learned she had gone on her own. He said it was too dangerous for a woman to be riding alone across the prairie, especially when she was intentionally riding to an Indian camp. It had been one of the only times in their marriage that they had fought.

Sarah stood by the pig pen, dumping leftovers into the trough while Gabriel pulled at bits of weeds in the yard. He was crawling now. His hair was growing in thick and dark on top of his head. An unhappy squeal came from his tiny lungs as a worm wriggled across his chubby fingers. Sarah laughed and picked him up, knocking the worm off of him. He clung to her apron for comfort as she soothed him. Across the prairie, an unfamiliar coach jostled towards Fort Marshall. Ruts and rocks knocked against its wheels, shaking it from side to side. The horses were as black as ink. Their manes were stray pen strokes in the wind. Sarah hoisted Gabriel higher on her hip as she watched the wagon bump and jump across the grassy plains. She picked up the slop bucket with her free hand and brushed a stray hair from her face.

The coach's wood had been painted red with gold filigree. One piece of luggage was strapped to the top. As the stagecoach rumbled by, a pale woman peeled back the curtain and peered out at Sarah and the baby. Her hair was almost as red as the coach. Her stare made Sarah uneasy. The woman closed the curtain again once the wagon was passed them. Sarah's heart beat rapidly, even though she wasn't quite sure why. Gabriel picked up on the change in her mood and started to cry. Sarah rocked him gently and whispered sweetly to him as she tried to get her own emotions under control. The bucket banged against her hip as she took the baby inside.

Around dinner time, Jacob came back from helping the Heely boys learn to read. They had to spend most of their time working the farm, since their pa died. Jacob and Miss Adams took turns tutoring them so they wouldn't fall too far behind the other kids in town.

Jake slid out of his boots and scooped Gabe up from where he was playing on the floor. He plopped down on his stool while waiting for

Sarah to fix his plate like she did every night. "How was my boy today?" He looked down at Gabriel while he bounced him on his knee.

"He was an absolute angel, weren't you?" Sarah slid Jacob's plate to him and reached over the table to touch Gabe's nose with her forefinger. He giggled at her touch. "Hey, did you see that stagecoach that rolled into town this afternoon?" She tried to sound less interested than she was as she brought it up.

"Uh, yeah," Jacob was distracted with the baby, "it was someone from Bakersfield, I think."

"Why would someone from Bakersfield come all the way out here?" Sarah played with the stew in her bowl as she talked.

Jacob took a bite of his dinner and chewed contemplatively, "I think she was looking for someone. Doc is letting her stay at his place since the two rooms above the General Store are currently full. I saw them chatting on my way back."

"I hope she's not here long."

"Sarah," Jacob's spoon clattered into his bowl, "that is not the way we need to act towards strangers. We need to make them feel welcome."

Sarah tilted her head down in shame. She nodded slowly, and they finished the rest of their meal in silence.

The rooster crowed, welcoming the sun the next day. Jacob and Sarah got dressed as Gabriel dozed back to sleep. A knock trilled on the doorframe. Gabe fussed at the sound of the noise.

Jacob's boots thudded heavily as he walked to the door and opened it, "Oh hey, Doc, come on in. Where is that lodger of yours this morning?"

"Mrs. Canady is fixing her some breakfast. Actually, that's what I came to talk to you about." Doc ran his callused hands over his whiskered face, "Sarah, Jacob, I think you two should probably sit down."

Sarah's stomach dropped. Her hands shook as she took a seat. She clasped her fingers tightly in her lap trying to hide her nervous quivering, "What is it?" Her voice was a trembling whisper.

"The woman who came into town yesterday was looking for her husband and her child. The descriptions she gave match that of the man who died in the carriage and of Gabriel."

Doc's words felt like a punch in the gut to Sarah. She couldn't breathe. Her hand flew to her chest, "No. It's not true."

Jacob walked behind his wife and placed his hands on her shoulders. "How do we know she's telling the truth?"

Doc fiddled in his pocket and pulled out an oval, gold locket. He opened it and handed it to Sarah, "She also had this."

The locket had a black and white photo of the man from the wreckage on one side, and a picture of baby Gabriel on the other. Sarah's trembling hand covered her mouth as she looked at the pictures. Tears began to fall down her cheeks silently. "No, please no." She looked up at her husband pleadingly.

"Sarah, if she is his mother, we have to give him back." Jacob held her head close to him as she cried. "If he had been your child, and you had lost him—"

"He is my child!" Sarah cried out as she stood up and pulled away from her husband. She picked up the baby and held him close. The familiar warmth of his breath in the curve of her neck deepened the ache in her heart.

"I've talked to her, and she has agreed to give you the rest of the day to say your goodbyes. You'll need to bring the baby by my place around sundown." Doc had given up trying to talk to Sarah. He focused his words on Jacob now who nodded in understanding.

"Thank you, Doc." Jake handed him back the locket. He fought back his own tears as Doc Brannigan excused himself from their home. After they had sat on the bed for a moment in mournful silence, Jake spoke up with false optimism, "Let's just take today to enjoy him a little more, ok?"

Sarah was rocking gently back and forth, "I don't know if I can do it, Jake. I don't know if I can give him up."

"I'll be there with you. We can do it together." He pulled her into him, and for a moment they tried to pretend their happy little family would last forever.

Dusk came far too quickly. There were so many laughs and new discoveries that they would never get to experience together. Sarah's eyes were red and puffy from hours of crying. Gabriel tried to make her smile, but each time he did, her smile would morph back into sobs.

"It's time." Jacob helped her to her feet.

Sarah's legs were numb as she carried Gabe towards the door. She walked with Jacob towards Doc's tiny home that often doubled as his clinic. "Oh no," she turned solemnly to her husband, "we forgot his blanket. He can't sleep without it." Slight panic rang from her throat.

"It's ok. I'll go back and get it for him." Jake kissed her cheek and turned to go get the blanket.

Sarah eased up to Doc's porch trying to steel her nerves. Through the murky window pane, she could see the red headed woman standing over Doc who was sitting in a chair. The woman straddled him and pulled his face up towards hers. As Sarah stood there watching, a silvery light began to lift from inside of Doc. The woman leaned down to kiss him. As her lips met his, the light went into her. His body grew pale and limp as she pulled away from him. Doc fell with a sickening thud to the floor.

Backing away from the window as quickly as she could, Sarah stumbled over an old milk pale that had been left by the porch. The clattering brought Sarah to her senses. She saw Maggie tied up on a post. Her fingers fought to undo the knot and hang on to Gabe at the same time. As Sarah swung herself up into the saddle, the woman came outside. For a split second, Sarah could have sworn that her eyes were as black as coal, but then they switched to an ordinary shade of green. Sarah dug her heels into Maggie's flanks. The old horse wasn't used to being treated so roughly, and she broke out in a startled run.

"No!" The woman screeched at the top of her lungs as Sarah rode away.

Sarah's only thought was that she had to get away. She couldn't let that woman have Gabriel. Maggie's steps were becoming uneven as she ran, but Sarah urged her forward. She glanced behind her. In the distance, she could see a dark horse in pursuit. The rider's red hair flamed in the sunset's light. By some instinct, Sarah felt driven to the Kiowa's tribe. She held Gabriel in one hand and the reins in the other, praying that Maggie wouldn't give up just yet.

As the teepees came into view, Sarah looked behind her once more. The other rider was gaining on them. Maggie was struggling now. Sarah rode into the middle of the camp and slid off of her borrowed horse. Pale Sparrow rushed out of her teepee to see what the commotion was about. The braves were gathered in a circle around a fire. Their faces were painted, and they danced wildly around the flames. Sarah hid behind Pale Sparrow as the red haired woman stopped her horse on the edge of the camp.

"The child is mine!" The woman's voice rang out over the camp. "He is owed to me." She stepped brazenly towards Sarah. Her voice seemed melodic, almost mesmerizing.

At the sound of her voice, Wandering Coyote emerged from his dwelling. He was chanting and carrying tobacco leaves. He made his way to the fire the braves were dancing around, and he cast the leaves into the flames. As the smell filled the air, the red haired woman backed away as if the scent was casting her back. She looked dazed as she blinked through the smoke. A few braves that had not been dancing circled around behind the woman and cried out as they caught her by the wrists and ankles. She tried to kick free, but they held her fast. Her eyes morphed back into black, soulless pits as her anger swelled.

Two of the men by her feet pulled off her shoes. Sarah gasped. Beneath the shoes, the woman's feet were cloven hooves. She kicked with more vigor, trying to break free from their grasp.

Wandering Coyote spoke in his native tongue, and Pale Sparrow translated for Sarah as he spoke, "You have been seen. Deer Woman, you have no more power of these people. Your face is known. Your spell is broken. You are cast out."

The woman screamed in agony as the braves released her. She mounted her black stallion and stormed off into the darkness. Soon not even her hair was visible on the horizon. Sarah had stood in shock through the entire process. She clutched Gabriel so tightly that her fingers were turning white.

"What just happened?" She was shaking as she faced Pale Sparrow.

"That was a Deer Woman. They feed on the souls of men. In your stories she would be called a Succubus. Wandering Coyote saw her in a vision. He knew she would come. Tobacco smoke drives them away, but the only way to send one away for good is to look at her cloven feet. In the old stories past down, it is said that the Deer Woman will mate with a man and have his baby. Once the child is born, she must sacrifice it to maintain her youth. If she is unable to do so, or if her identity is revealed before she can complete the sacrifice, she will become mortal."

"What about the baby?" Sarah looked down at Gabriel, "Will he become like her?"

"Our stories only ever speak of Deer Women. We do not have any tales about Deer Men." Pale Sparrow rested her hand on Gabriel's head with a smile.

Sarah breathed a small sigh of relief. She was still trembling. Wandering Coyote walked over and took one of Sarah's hands in his. He brought her and the baby near the fire as the smoke billowed up. He chanted and wafted the smoke over her and Gabriel as he sang. After a few moments a young boy brought Maggie over to her. Sarah nodded in gratitude.

"He has put a blessing around you and the baby." Pale Sparrow gestured to a few braves who had mounted their own horses, "They will accompany you to your village to make sure you make it back safe."

"Thank you." A tear of gratefulness fell down Sarah's cheek as she climbed back on Maggie and rode towards Fort Marshall.

The Kiowa hung back as the town came into view. Sarah finished the ride to her home alone. Jacob was waiting on the porch for her. He ran to greet her. As he held her in his arms, he said, "I was worried sick about you. What happened?"

Sarah recounted what she had seen at Doc's and what had happened with the tribe. Jacob said that he had seen the woman ride out of town and had found Doc dead in his own home. There were no signs of struggle or foul play. It looked as if he had died from natural causes. That night, Sarah and Jacob both stayed awake. The events of the night kept them from their dreams.

The next day, Jacob held the funeral service for Doc. Everyone turned up to reminisce about his loving and helpful nature. Only Sarah and Jacob knew the truth about how he had died. They didn't want to sully his memory with what had really happened. As they bowed their heads to pray a parting prayer over his grave, one of the little girls in the town locked eyes with Gabriel, and for a split second, she thought she saw them go completely black.

COLD ANGEL

OLIVIA BRAUN

The world felt as if it was closing in on the car as Daniel steered them through icy forest roads. Rachel watched as the light snow and fog got thicker and thicker as they ascended. She wasn't worried. She didn't worry about much anymore. And she didn't miss the view. Her body was on its way to her parents' lakeside cabin on December twentieth - very much against their advice - but her mind was trapped six months in the past, in her home in the small town of Lovelock, Nevada, as it had been ever since her daughter was found face-down and motionless in the bathtub.

"This is a good idea," Daniel said. He wiped dirt off the inside of his glasses with his finger, trying to keep his eyes on the road which was lined either side with enormous, snow-blanketed fir trees. "We've got more than enough supplies to last us a month if we get stuck up here."

It was a terrible idea, Rachel thought. But she let him think that he was helping. She didn't care where she was, truthfully, and was under no illusions that the untimely death of her five-year-old daughter would upset her less after a change of scenery. At least it would save them a little money on rent, she thought. Since Kayleigh died, they hadn't been able to sleep in their house. Money was tight before, but even with a loan from her parents, they were about to hit real trouble.

"There's something up ahead," Daniel said. "This is it, right?"

Rachel sat up a little and squinted. She could make out the shape of it through the fog. It was a two-storey cabin with shutters over the small windows, an old swing-chair hanging on the porch and a wooden deer sculpture out front. The roof was covered with a thick layer of snow and the wooden deer was up to his knees in it. It was only three in the afternoon, but between the snow storm and the fog, it was already getting dark. The car's headlights struggled to pick out the cabin through the snow as they got nearer. The cabin took on more features and color as they drove into the fog. The car, a Toyota four-by-four, pushed through the snow and came to a stop with its lights shining through the windows of the cabin. Rachel hadn't seen the place since she was a teenager.

"It hasn't changed a bit," she said, feeling almost disappointed. "I thought it would look different now, but it's exactly how I remember it."

Daniel left the engine running so they could enjoy the heaters for a few precious minutes before heading outside. Rachel sat and let her mind wander to when she was fifteen, without a care in the world, chasing her sister around the forest with a water gun. Rachel missed her sister terribly. She didn't really miss the person her sister had become, the high-flying attorney who had packed up her husband and three kids for Australia five years ago. She missed the girl she had shared her childhood with, rather than the adult who poked her here and there with phone calls from the other side of the world. Rachel missed the girl that she once was, too, and the world she once lived in.

Rachel started a little when Daniel took her hand.

"It can be like it was," he said. "You just need some time away. You've been doing too much. You need to relax."

Rachel said nothing.

She wasn't convinced.

The cabin looked the same, but inside it was emptier, darker.

Just like me, Rachel thought.

*

Rachel kneeled over the fire and prodded it to get it going, her icy breath floating in front of her face, as Daniel was out back gassing up the generator. The fire was slowly coming alive and filling the musty room with a warm, unsteady glow and Rachel looked around. The bare floorboards were freezing under her knees and the floor, as with everything from what she could make out, was covered with a light coating of dust. The lounge was spacious and furnished with floral-patterned furniture that would have been considered luxurious in the eighties. Rachel had considered it luxurious in the eighties. The bookshelf, her father's favorite hideaway on their summer vacations, was still stocked with reserve copies of everything he had at home. There were psychology reference books, reports and a smattering of fiction - DeLillo and Ballard, mostly - which, as a child, she'd found incomprehensible. In the bottom corner of the bookshelf was a small pile of C.S. Lewis and J.R.R. Tolkien he had bought for Rachel and her sister to keep them quiet, to lessen the more destructive or noisy games that disturbed his reading.

Something moved in the top corner of the room, beyond the bookshelf. Rachel stood and grabbed a duster from the box on the floor. It was a cobweb, dangling from side to side. Wiping it away, she hoped that didn't mean spiders. It had been cold enough up here now that they should've all died out, she told herself.

French doors at the back of the room, past a small dining table, looked out onto a long stretch of snow with a small, now-bare apple tree protruding from it, like a black, skeletal hand reaching up from the earth itself. Rachel tried not to look at it. The tree had always unnerved her as a child. She could hear it rustling in the night as she lay awake in her bed trying to pretend she was safe and sound in Nevada. Past the tree was only a wall of shifting whiteness. The fog and the snow obscured completely Jackson Lake which lay beyond.

Rachel stood and watched the ebb and tide of the whiteness which surrounded the cabin and created for her and Daniel a physical barrier between them and the rest of the world. She was grateful for it - and she was sure her parents were grateful for it, having of late become visibly impatient with her relentless grief - but it also filled her with something approaching dread. She had spent the last six months in an unending fit of despair, one which she wasn't sure she would ever see the other side of. There had been nights when she had convinced herself that her life was over, that it was only a matter of moments before she found the courage to take her own life. But she was still here. She was functioning.

She wasn't entertaining those kinds of thoughts anymore. Entering this void of whiteness, a hole in the weather in which she and Daniel could bury themselves, it felt like hiding. It felt like they were tunneling a safe-house for themselves, deep and far from the rest of the world. Rachel was scared that it would take a considerable effort to pull herself out of this tunnel, and worried that she wouldn't have the strength or the will to do it. They had taken themselves out of the world, essentially, and she didn't know if she would want to go back.

The front door slammed shut and startled her out of her gloomy daydream. She took a breath and rubbed the back of her neck.

"Did you get it going?" she said. "The lights are still off."

She turned and peered into the darkness of the hallway through the open lounge door.

"Dan?" she said.

She heard him kicking the wall to knock the snow off his shoes, but it was too dark to see him with only the small fire to light the place. She walked over to the door.

"Did you find my dad's gas store?" she said. "He said there should be enough there to keep us in as much electricity as we can eat for a few months if it comes to it."

She heard him walked up the stairs, but he didn't speak. Frowning, Rachel walked into the dark hallway.

"Dan?" she said, looking up the stairs. "Where are you going?"

She saw a shadow turn the corner at the top of the stairs as she peered up from the bottom.

"You're not going to help me with these freakin' boxes?"

The silence made her uneasy.

What the hell is his problem? she thought.

"Daniel," she called up. "What are you doing?"

There was no response. She held onto the railing, thinking about following him up into the dark upper floor. Something about him being in the dark up there in silence made her stomach turn. He had been distraught about Kayleigh's death, too, but he had recovered. He had been strong for Rachel. His grief was the quiet kind, the detached kind, not like Rachel's, wailing, dribbling and hitting herself periodically for months on end. Rachel's grief was ugly, she knew that. But never for a moment had Daniel been anything less than her own personal therapist and cheerleader. She couldn't ask any more of him. His silence now was getting to her.

"Daniel," she called up again.

She took a few deep breaths and took the first step up the stairs.

Something screeched outside and the cabin was suddenly filled with harsh, white light. Rachel covered her eyes and curled up. Her heart dropped in her chest and she was overcome with panic.

She heard the front door slam behind her and she turned quickly around.

Daniel was stood in the doorway with a grin on his face.

"I got it..." he started, but the panic on Rachel's face stopped him in his tracks. "What's wrong, Rach?" he said.

Rachel looked up the stairs. The upper floor looked empty. She didn't speak for a moment, listening for movement.

"What is it?" Daniel said. He kicked the snow off his shoes and moved to embrace Rachel.

Rachel put up a hand and said, "Were you just in here?"

Daniel looked confused. "What? No," he said. "I was getting the generator going." He pointed to the working lights and said, "See?"

"I thought I heard you come in," Rachel said.

She looked up the stairs. Daniel's face hardened. He looked up the stairs, too.

"Stay here," he said.

"Wait," Rachel said, reaching out after him as he walked quickly up the stairs, his boots knocking hard on the wooden slats.

He reached the top of the stairs and looked around. Rachel waited with bated breath. He walked away from the top of the stairs and

Rachel listened to his boots on the floorboards. She heard him opening doors, entering rooms, walking around. Rachel put her hand through her hair and tried to calm herself. She leaned against the wall. Something cold and wet made her move her hand away. It was water. She looked at the wall and saw in a faint outline, half destroyed by her touching it, the wet outline of a small hand on the yellow-beige floral wallpaper.

She took a step back and brought her hand to her mouth. Tears hit her eyes and her lungs locked down and stopped her breath.

It was a child's hand-print, still wet.

It was still dripping down the wall, and after a few seconds, it had become a shapeless, watery mark.

The sound of Daniel's footsteps grew louder and he appeared at the top of the stairs.

"There's no-one up here," he said, walking back down. "You sure you heard something?"

Rachel looked at him with tears in her eyes. She swallowed hard and glanced at him to the now-unrecognizable wet spot on the wall.

"What's wrong?" he said, embracing her.

She let herself get lost in his arms and closed her eyes. She started to breathe again.

You're being a freakin' idiot, she told herself. You've lost it. Get yourself together, woman.

"What is it?" he said. "Is it this place? I know it's a little spooky in the dark with the storm and all, but we'll make it cozy, you'll see." He moved back and took her face in his cold hands and looked at her with concern. "Are you OK?" he said.

Rachel dried her eyes and nodded. She attempted a smile. "I just got a little spooked, I guess," she said. "I'm sorry. I'm being childish."

Daniel hugged her close.

"I love you," Rachel said.

"More than anything," Daniel replied, as was their routine.

*

The first night was passing slowly. Rachel and Daniel lay in bed facing in opposite directions, not touching, not speaking, waiting to fall asleep, just like they had done every other night in recent memory. When they were awake and walking around in the daylight, Rachel had moments where she felt things were almost as they were before. She could never pretend Kayleigh was just in the next room - the constant and intense longing in her gut would never go away - but things between her and Daniel at times could be described as normal. He could be charming and loving and kind. He couldn't be funny again yet, even though he'd started trying recently. But when the sun went down and they lay in bed together with nothing but their thoughts, Rachel could hardly bring herself to say his name or look him in the eye. Maybe he felt the same way.

But I wasn't the one who let her drown, Rachel thought.

She closed the thought down almost as soon as she had it. It wasn't healthy, she knew that. It wasn't anyone's fault, that's what she kept telling herself. But, deep down, there was a dark place inside her reserved for such thoughts.

It had been Daniel's turn to give Kayleigh a bath. Rachel could hear her laughing and playing for a while. He was telling her a story about a friendly monster. Rachel fell asleep with a book in her hands. When it dropped from her grasp and hit the floor, it woke her up. There was no laughter to be heard, then. The silence made her feel sick to her stomach, before she'd even known what had happened. When she walked into the bathroom, Kayleigh was face-down in the water. She'd slipped and bumped her head, that's what they said. She was unconscious as the water filled her little lungs. Rachel didn't know what happened after that. She has flashes of memory here and there, of blue lips and cold hands, but nothing substantial to hold onto. She didn't know where Daniel was. She didn't know what she did. She woke up in the hospital. Daniel said he had just stepped away for two minutes, that she was safe when he left her.

But she wasn't safe.

If she was safe, Rachel thought, she wouldn't have drowned.

Rachel lay on her side in bed. The moon was reflecting off the snow outside and it gave the room a light glow. Rachel's eyes were wide open. She was tired, but she couldn't sleep. All she could do, as on any other night, was lay there and think, if she was safe then she wouldn't have drowned.

Rachel slipped the covers off her and wrapped a bathrobe around her on top of her pajamas. She kicked on her slippers and walked downstairs in search of a hot drink.

The light in the kitchen blinded Rachel when she flipped it on. She covered her eyes and stood still for a moment to let her tired eyes adjust. She started making herself a cup of cocoa and she studied her reflection in the night-blackened windows. She had bags under her eyes and her long, auburn hair was a tangled mess. She looked at herself long enough to realize that she couldn't see anything on the outside. The windows were open to the outside world but acted only as dark mirrors for those inside. The thought made Rachel's blood run cold.

Rachel's feet ran cold too. Turning, she saw that the back door had come open slightly and was drifting ever more open with the breeze. The snow storm had calmed, thankfully, but it was still freezing outside. Rachel pushed the door closed gently so as to not wake Daniel. She looked at the cuckoo clock on the wall. It was three in the morning. Rachel stirred her cocoa and took the kettle off the stove. When she flipped off the light switch, she saw a straight line of moonlight coming from behind her.

The back door was ajar again.

Nothing to worry about, Rachel said. I just didn't close it tightly, that's all. That's all it is.

Rachel placed her cocoa down on the kitchen table and walked across the tiled floor to the back door, her slippers scraping as she dragged her feet. Touching the handle of the door, she looked out. Now that it was dark inside, she could see outside.

There was nothing there, just snow and moonlight and the big black hand that was the dead apple tree.

Rachel pushed the door closed gently until it clicked. She took the key from off a hook on the wall to lock it shut. She pressed the key into the lock, but it was stiff. Jangling it, it still wouldn't go.

"Come on," Rachel whispered.

She crouched down and looked inside the keyhole. It was dark. There didn't seem to be anything blocking the way. She took the large key and guided it in with both hands, making completely sure not to twitch or tremble. She didn't want it to go off course. Once the key was in firmly, completely, she turned it slowly and with a small clunk it was locked.

"That wasn't so hard, was it?" she said to herself.

Standing up, she saw a small, pale face peering up from the bottom of the back door window.

Rachel recoiled and fell onto her back, knocking the wind out of herself.

She looked up at the back door window and the face peered over the bottom frame at her with large black eyes. Rachel tried to scream, but her breath hadn't come back. She fumbled around behind her for the light switch. The back door handle was being turned from outside, rattled.

Rachel spun around, flipped the kitchen light on and turned back to the door.

The face was gone.

Rachel caught her breath and didn't blink.

In the light, she could see now the window pane had misted up under where the face had been, under where its breath had come into contact with the glass. Something was written in the condensation, a word smudged into the moisture with a small finger.

Rachel took a tentative step forward to read what it said.

It said: D A D D Y

*

By the time her screaming had woken Daniel and he'd gotten downstairs, the word had faded on the glass.

"I saw someone," Rachel said, pointing from where she sat on the floor with her knees tucked up to her chest. "It was a little kid, I think. There at the back door. Looking in."

Daniel kneeled on the floor beside her and held her. "There's no-one out here, honey," he said. "We're in the middle of nowhere. There's no one else for miles around. It's OK, hush now."

"I saw it," she said.

Daniel kissed her on the forehead and looked her in the eyes as if searching for the truth in there.

"I saw it," she repeated.

Daniel and Rachel didn't sleep for the rest of the night. Daniel stayed up until dawn with her. Neither spoke, but rather sat and read on opposite sides of the room. Daniel was comforting when he spoke, but the fact that he rarely spoke belied his real feelings. He looked almost angry, Rachel thought. There was a tension there, just under the surface. He smiled a little too easily, spoke a little too calmly. Dawn came at long last and with it, Rachel and Daniel prepared breakfast and planned their day. In the light of day, Rachel's fears about the place died away. She walked out to the lake through the back door and didn't give the dead apple tree a second glance. She didn't look for strangers or jump at animal sounds. She simply walked to the lake to see if it had changed.

Jackson Lake sat in the shadow of the magnificent Teton mountains. In the icy weather, they looked like death incarnate, promising only starvation and frost-bite and a painful end in grand isolation. The lake was sealed with a thin sheet of ice which twinkled in the sunlight and the surrounding forests were white with their trees bent and misshapen from the weight of the snow.

Rachel dug in the snow for a moment and dug up a large stone. Walking to the edge of the lake, she threw the stone and listened to it crack through the ice further in and splash as it sank into the depths of the lake.

She stood for a moment and enjoyed the silence. She took a baby step forward and let the water that was coming out from under the cracked ice at the edge touch the bottom of her boots. The cold was creeping through her wool gloves and she started to feel a slow pain coming on, the raw stinging of the water from the snow seeping onto her skin. Rachel thought about how it would feel if that was all over her body, how bad the pain would be and how long it would last if she threw herself into the lake.

The wind rushed through the nearby trees and Rachel closed her eyes and listened to the sound of the branches scraping up against one another. In the noise, she thought she heard words, faint, masked by the wind, or perhaps made from it.

"Dee-add," came the whisper. "Deeeeee-add."

Rachel closed her eyes tighter and listened hard. It was like someone was whispering on the wind, only not quite. It didn't sound like a person.

"Deeee-ad," it came clear as day.

Rachel opened her eyes. She heard it.

"Daddy," it whispered.

Suddenly, a hand touched her back. Rachel leaped around and swore.

"Daniel!" she said.

"Christ," he said. "I'm sorry. I called you. I thought you knew I was here."

He put his arms around her waist from behind and she faced the lake. She was tense. She looked around to see if anyone else was lurking.

I must be going crazy, she thought.

"What are you doing out here anyway?" he said.

"I was just looking," Rachel said, trying not to sound too scared.

"It's a beautiful place," Daniel said. "It could use a little sunshine, but it's real nice up here, don't you think?"

Daniel was holding her tight. A little too tight, Rachel thought.

"I could live up here, I think," Daniel said. "No crowds, no traffic, no noise, just us and mother nature."

Rachel turned in his arms and faced him. She tried to smile.

"You're right," Daniel said. "No internet. We'd hate it."

Daniel smiled, but there was something behind the smile. Rachel didn't know what it was. She'd never seen it before. It unnerved her. It was, again, as if his smile was too genuine, too easy. She used to be able to read him like an open book. Lately, for the past year or so, he'd constructed a wall. Rachel had no idea what went on in his head.

"We better head inside," Rachel said. "Looks like that storm's coming back."

Daniel didn't move. He just looked at her, thinking.

"Daniel?" she said.

He nodded and snapped out of whatever it was that had hold of his attention. "Let's go in," he said. "You're right. Let's batten down the hatches and make that fire earn its keep." He laughed as he took her hand and they walked away from the shore of the lake. His laugh unsettled Rachel, but she didn't know why.

*

Rachel waited impatiently for the night to come. She and Daniel sat by the fire and read, talking very little. She read her dog-eared C.S. Lewis while he poured over her father's textbooks. She wanted to be rid of Daniel and his odd stares and long silences. She wanted to go back out to the lake. Whatever it is, she thought, it's out there. And it's trying to talk to me.

Craziness be damned, she thought. If I'm crazy, I'm crazy, but I have to see.

There was a small part of her that hoped beyond all hope that maybe, just maybe, it was Kayleigh. Rachel had never put much faith in the supernatural or religion, but she had always held out a little bit of hope that there was something else, after all this. Now, having lost the light of her life, she had more hope than ever.

But why would Kayleigh come to her now, after all this time? And why here?

"I think I'm going to head up to bed," Daniel said, yawning and snapping his book closed. "Are you coming?"

Rachel tried to look calm. She smiled as warmly as she could manage. "I'm gonna stay up for a bit longer," she said. "I want to read some more."

"Trapped in Narnia," Daniel said as he kissed her on the top of her head. "Don't stay up too long, hey? I'm just upstairs if you need anything."

"OK," Rachel said.

The next wait was the longest of all. Rachel timed herself. She would wait two hours before going outside. Daniel was sure to be asleep by then. She tried to distract herself with the book, but while her eyes did move over the words none of them entered her mind. Her thoughts were racing. She felt nauseous with worry about herself, about her mental health.

This is how it starts, she thought. It seems a little weird, but you accept it. Then it gets weirder and weirder and you accept it easier and easier until one day you're dressed all in white and lining up for pills in your ward in the nut house.

The clock in the lounge was a smiling Felix the cat. His whiskers were the hands. Rachel had begged her dad to buy that clock one summer when she was a girl. It had taken three whole days to persuade him, and just as long again to persuade him to put it up in the lounge. Rachel stared at Felix until his face was burned onto the back of her eyeballs. His whiskers moved painfully slowly, tick tick ticking along.

Rachel must have dozed off, because after a long blink, it was time. It was three in the morning. Daniel had been upstairs for four hours. There's no way he's awake, Rachel thought.

She pulled on her big winter coat with the fur hood, slipped into her boots, and walked into the kitchen. She turned off the kitchen light before she moved to the back door. It looked lonely outside. It was only in the dark that the isolation of the place really hit Rachel. They were hundreds and hundreds of miles from anyone. Daniel said he hoped she could rest easier, but, if anything, it was making things worse.

Here I am, she thought, walking out into a snow storm at three in the morning looking for ghosts. I have absolutely cracked up.

She opened the door slowly and silently. The snow had piled up a little at the door, the wind having blown it against the house. Rachel looked around with her icy breath hanging in front of her face. She looked beyond the black hand of the apple tree, to the forest beyond, and she squinted to try to see through the light but constant and swirling snowfall to Jackson Lake, but she couldn't. Rachel stepped outside and closed the door, listening for the click of the catch.

The moon was full and bright and the snow-covered ground glowed in its rays. Dark spots in the snow caught Rachel's eye. There were two of them, right in front of her. Rachel covered her eyes with her gloved hands and looked down.

Her heart almost stopped.

Footprints.

It was a pair of child's footprints.

No bigger or smaller than Kayleigh's were, Rachel thought.

She took a deep breath and took a step forward in the direction of the lake, where the footprints were pointing. And as she stepped another set of footprints appeared in front of her. She kept walking, and step after step revealed child's footsteps in front of her. She was being led.

Looking up, peering through the snow, Rachel caught a glimpse of a child running away, its arms flapping by its sides as it ran as fast as it could. It looked back over its shoulder.

It was Kayleigh.

Rachel stopped and dropped to her knees. She was overcome with joy, just seeing her daughter's face.

Kayleigh looked scared.

"Daddy!" Rachel heard her call.

Rachel stood and ran as fast as she could through the snow. The storm was beginning to calm and the half-frozen lake appeared in front of her out of the fog. Kayleigh was gone, but her footprints led to the water. Rachel looked around, panicked.

"Kayleigh," she said. "Kayleigh, please."

"Daddy," a whisper came behind her.

Rachel spun around and was facing the cabin. No-one was stood behind her, but as the storm subsided and the fog drifted away, Rachel could see the cabin clearly. In the bedroom window, Daniel stood watching her.

"Daniel?" Rachel said.

He was fully dressed in his coat, hat, and gloves. He was completely motionless, utterly expressionless. His eyes were locked on Rachel. In the glow of the moon, his face was totally white, and his eyes were deep in shadow. He stared down at Rachel with something that looked like contempt. She had never seen any expression even resembling it on his face before.

He looked like he hated her.

He's been waiting up this whole time, Rachel suddenly thought. But why?

"Daddy," came the voice behind her.

Rachel turned and suddenly, there was Kayleigh, stood with her feet in the icy water of the lake.

"Daddy," she said.

"Baby," Rachel said. She reached out to touch her but stopped just short from fear of making her leave.

"Daddy," she said again.

Rachel started to lose all feeling in her body, starting with her hands. They tingled and then went dead. A feeling of horror swept over her as she started to lose all control of herself as if possessed. Her hands moved forwards of their own accord.

"Wait," Rachel said. "No."

Her hands grabbed hold of Kayleigh, holding her by her shoulders. Rachel fought it with every fiber of her being, but she wasn't in control.

"Daddy," Kayleigh said, "what are you doing?"

Rachel heard her own voice say, "Hush, baby. This won't hurt."

Rachel pushed Kayleigh down in the water. She didn't fight. She smiled, thinking they were playing a game.

"Daddy," she said again, "what-"

Her head was pushed under the water. She barely struggled. Rachel's hands held her there. Kayleigh hardly moved. She trusted it was a game, right until the moment before she passed out when there was a small flash of panic and a muffled scream. And then she was drowned.

"No," Rachel said. "No, no, no."

Her hands wouldn't move. They held Kayleigh's lifeless body down in the icy water.

"Let me go!" she screamed, and suddenly her hands were released.

Rachel fell backward into the snow, screaming and crying. It was him, she thought. He did it on purpose! He drowned her! He drowned her with his own hands! That's what she wanted to show me!

"Rachel," the voice came from behind her.

She turned and stood. He offered his hand, but she didn't take it.

"What are you doing out here?" he said.

Rachel sniffed back her tears.

"I, uh, couldn't sleep," he said. "And I saw you thrashing around out here. You're worrying me, honey."

Rachel couldn't find the words to speak.

"You're worrying everyone," he said. "They don't know what you might do to yourself."

That was it, she thought. That was why now, why here. He'd brought her out here to kill her, to make it look like she'd finally had enough and taken her own life. It was a warning. "Daddy," she said. She was warning her.

"Rachel," he said, "I'm talking to you."

"Stay away from me," she whispered. "I know what you are."

Confused, he nearly laughed. "Rachel, I don't know what you mean. What am I?"

"I know what you did," she said.

His half-smile dropped. He became serious. "What did I do?" he said.

Rachel took a step back and looked behind her. She was on the edge of the lake, her boots in the water.

"It's so quiet up here, isn't it?" he said, taking a step towards her. "You could get away with anything up here."

"Why did you do it?" Rachel said, bursting into tears. Then, screaming, she said, "You drowned her! Why?!"

"I don't know!" he shouted back, leaning towards her. "You don't have reasons for things like this!"

Rachel looked at him, stunned.

"I was going to kill us all," he said, quieter. "I can't take this world anymore. I was going to kill us all, so we could be together. We could finally be as happy as we deserve to be."

Rachel broke down in tears and said, "Kayleigh was happy!"

Daniel wiped tears away from his own eyes and stepped towards Rachel.

"Stay away!" she screamed.

Daniel grabbed her arm with one hand and with the other took out a hunting knife from a sheath under his coat. "Nobody will understand," he said. "Nobody really cares anyway. We're better off this way."

"No!" Rachel screamed. "You're fucking insane!"

She punched and kicked at Daniel, splashing in the water, but he held her still and brought the knife against her chest, the point over her heart. "Hush, baby," he said. "This won't hurt."

A small voice came from behind Daniel. "Daddy," it said.

Daniel turned, and in that moment Rachel grabbed his knife, twisted it back and plunged it deep into his stomach. He screamed for his life and fell to his knees. Rachel stepped away, leaving the knife inside him, as he dropped onto his hands and knees in the water, turning back towards the cabin. In front of him stood Kayleigh. The icy water turned red around him as he looked at his dead daughter in utter terror.

Rachel moved to the shore and watched as he shook his head. "No," he said. He looked at Rachel and said, "Come with me. Be with us." Blood spilled out of his mouth and he collapsed face down in the water.

"You're going to a different place," Rachel said.

Daniel's body went limp in the water. Rachel heard his dying breath, a long final exhalation. And he was gone.

"Mummy," a voice came, and with that Kayleigh vanished into a flurry of snow carried on the wind.

The storm was coming back. The clouds were drawing in overhead, shutting out the moonlight. The world was getting darker, but Rachel felt herself straightening up, the fog of grief lifting from her mind.

She trudged back through the snow as it got heavier and heavier. Slamming the back door behind her, she felt entirely closed off from everyone. The cabin was consumed by the storm. Rachel sat on the kitchen floor with her back to the wall. And though she started to cry, she was filled with this unshakable feeling the likes of which she hadn't felt for years, not since the day Kayleigh was born. Rachel felt that even if the storm worsened, she would be able to survive it.

She could survive anything.

The End.

WE ALL FALL DOWN

TAMI BARRERA

Chapter One

In every movie he'd seen, Mark Allen Geer noticed that spooky hospitals and corridors were always darker than they should have been. Why was that? He didn't realize the fact until he entered the halls of Fern Heights Rehabilitation and Assisted Living.

He set his large hands on the wheels of his chair and stopped its motion forward. He looked around and over his shoulder when the chair jogged forward. An attendant had stumbled into him when he'd abruptly stopped.

"Sorry, sir. I didn't mean to run into you."

Mark ran his eyes up the blue scrubs to the sheepish face of the young attendant. His mood told him to scowl fiercely and cuss the young man out. But for once, he didn't. He clenched his jaw, nodded and turned back around.

"Why is it so dark in here?" He asked loudly. "Where's the lights? Why does it have to be so dark?"

"This is only temporary, sir." The attendant, whose name was Josh, said in a respectful voice. Mark tried not to like him. He'd been forced to come to this rehab. He'd just returned from his third tour in Iraq, each one extended to the maximum amount of time allowed. He considered himself young. He would be turning 30 in a few months. His plan had always been to retire from the military and live in a small house somewhere yelling at kids to get off the lawn.

It had only come to an end because he'd been shot. It made him mad. It made him furious, to be completely honest. He had no family, having lost both his parents as a small child and raised by grandparents who were involved in a fatal car accident when he was about to graduate from high school.

He'd always been interested in the military. When his life took such a violent turn, he took advantage of the events and signed up for the Army. He wanted to be on the front lines. He wanted to be where all the action was, killing the enemy with precision.

He'd been doing just what he wanted, just what he loved to do, when the bullet from a hidden sniper up on the roof of a nearby building had entered his spine, severing it so precisely, there was no way to restore the use of his legs. He would never walk again. That put an end to his career in the military. He wasn't educated enough to have a job behind a desk. His body had been left a wreck after the shooting. His life changed forever.

He'd been an angry young man before entering the military. Now that his passion was ripped from his hands in the prime of his life, all he wanted to do was die.

That was what he'd told the hospital psychiatrist during their last session. Quickly after that, they'd shipped him here, where the government could keep a proper eye on him. They didn't want him to turn into another statistic. Just another returning injured veteran offing himself, handing over the ultimate sacrifice for his country.

He was proud of his country and did, in fact, fight to protect it. If he killed himself, it wouldn't be because he was mad about the war. It would be because he was mad he couldn't fight in it anymore.

He realized the attendant had continued speaking and focused in on his words, wondering how much he'd missed while stewing in his bitterness.

"...adjustments. They plan to be done with the remodeling in the next month. Until then, some of the lights are kept on in certain corridors because they are in the process of replacing the lamps."

Mark was satisfied he hadn't missed much. He stared down the corridor to the left and then to the right. This Victorian style home was massive. It had once been a prosperous plantation house. Now it served as the rehabilitation clinic for injured soldiers.

He moved through the foyer, easily wheeling around the reception desk, following Josh and the other attendant, a huge black man called Steven Long. Mark thought of a bouncer as soon as he saw the man.

But this wasn't a bar, there would be no alcohol and the nurses weren't as pretty as barmaids would be. And he didn't have to tip them.

"This is your room, Mr. Geer. It has been fitted with the equipment you'll need to make your stay more comfortable."

"I'm not going to get better," Mark grumbled without looking at either attendant. "So I think my stay is gonna be pretty long."

Josh just nodded, opening the door, going in and holding it open wide so Mark could get through. He looked around the room, slightly distracted by the thought that he could feel a headache coming on and for some odd reason, his legs felt cold. He wasn't usually able to feel his legs at all. So the fact that they were cold made him confused.

"Okay, thanks. Thanks. This will be fine. I appreciate it. Okay." He made a wide circle with his chair and nodded as Steven and Josh brought in his trunk and two duffle bags. He eyed the small pile and sighed, realizing everything he owned in the world was packed in those three items.

Josh and Steven went back out the door. Josh turned back. "We'll be serving lunch in a half hour, sir. That should be enough time for you to get somewhat settled. If you would like to have lunch in here, that would suitable. Or would you care to go to the dining hall?"

"I'll go to the dining hall." Mark wanted to check out the other patients and the staff on duty. He'd never been to this rehab before. He'd never been shot before so there hadn't been a need for one. He wasn't going to isolate himself in this creepy room all the time. He needed to get out and explore. But first, he would look for possible enemies and cohorts. He would assess the situation and act accordingly, just like his favorite drill sergeant, Col. Drew Baxter-Hall, who yelled at him all the way through boot camp so long ago, had advised him to do on every mission he went on.

Chapter Two

He closed the door behind the two attendants and pushed the wheels on his chair so that he rolled backwards slightly. He stared at the room around him. It had been modernized but the wallpaper gave away its age. The entire building was built in 1923 and totally remodeled twice, once in 1976 and once in 2006. Mark was slightly annoyed that in the second remodeling, they hadn't bothered to put up new wallpaper. Or paneling. Anything would have been better than the same old wallpaper from the seventies. A strange greenish brown color. Not even anything cheerful. At the very least, colors that didn't remind him of the dusty plains in Iraq. Brown. Brown everywhere. All shades of it.

He shook his head and wheeled over to the edge of the bed. He pushed himself out of the chair and onto the bed, using the motion of the bouncing bed to pull his legs up and stretch them out in front of him. The bed groaned a little. It was unnerving. There was no reason for it to make any sounds. He was a big man but not *that* big. He weighed a steady 185 at his most muscular, standing 5'11".

He looked down at the bed. The sound of groaning continued but was faded...muffled...

His heart pounded harder. Was the sound coming from under the bed? He felt stupid. There were no monsters under the bed.

"You're not going stir-crazy, Mark. It's not going to happen. There's no monsters under the bed. There's no danger in this room. That's why you're here. Remember? So you can't do yourself any harm."

He kept mumbling comforting words as his heart hammered in his chest and he leaned over slowly to look at the floor beside the bed. He wouldn't see anything, he knew that. He wouldn't be able to lean over far enough to actually see under the bed anyway.

He felt like a fool, staring down at the thin yellow carpet. He was a grown man. Why was he so nervous? He sat back up straight, frustrated with himself. Now he didn't want to be on the bed. He wanted to be back in his chair. He wanted to go sit by the window and stare out at the landscape around the big house-turned-hospital. He wondered if his window faced the nearby woods or the parking lot.

With his luck, it would be the parking lot.

He scooted his body over and moved his legs so they were hanging off the edge of the bed, ignoring the fear that shot through him, picturing hands coming out from under the bed, grabbing his ankles and dragging him under. He yanked on the chair to drag it close again and pushed himself back from the bed to the chair.

Once he was settled in, he rolled to the window, blinking a few times at the bright light coming in from outside. His eyes adjusted to it quickly. He stared out with a blank expression, taking in as far into the distance as he could. He could only see a few people moving about on the lawn. It turned out he could see half of the yard and half of the parking lot. Beyond that he could see part of the street and the distance was lined with woods and mountains. That suited him fine. He was determined to try to find good things to focus on. There had to be something that would make this place a little less like Hell than it already appeared to be. He stared at the horizon, wishing he was a bird that could take flight and get out of this torment he was in.

He looked away from the window. The room was situated so that anything he needed was at waist level, his faucet, a small fridge set in the corner, the dresser was long and short, a full length mirror was attached to the back of the door. He was grateful to see the door to the bathroom slightly ajar. He was glad to have a bathroom in his room. That meant he didn't have to worry about going out into the common room to get to a community bathroom, like he'd had to at the last facility he was in.

He felt a rush of cold air and sucked in a quick deep breath of surprise. The hairs on his arm and the back of his neck stood on end. He shivered. Frowning, he stared around the room. There was something wrong...something felt *wrong*. He didn't want to be in there anymore. He pushed the chair forward forcefully and opened the door.

Just as he went through the doorway, he noticed a difference in how he felt. The headache that had been threatening him the entire time he was in the room almost immediately vanished. He could no longer feel his legs, cold *or* warm.

He rolled away from the door, glancing over his shoulder as it closed behind him. He narrowed his eyes.

"Mr. Geer, are you all right? Would you like a tour of the facilities while we wait for lunch to be put on the table?" He looked down the short hallway to a woman who was standing just behind the reception desk. She wasn't dressed casually like a receptionist. She was dressed like a nurse.

"Who are you?" he asked, trying not to sound blunt.

"My name is Barbara Prince. You can call me Babs. Everyone else does."

"All right, Babs. Yes," he nodded. "I'd like a tour of the facilities, thanks."

She gave him a smile that made him feel more comfortable than he had in a very long time. It was still too dark and he didn't like that. He didn't like the shadows that were cast by the shade in the hallway and down the corridors. But something in the woman's smile made him feel warm...peaceful. She went around his chair and grasped the handles, leaning forward to look at him. She smelled like strawberries.

Mark liked strawberries.

"I'll push you, Mr. Geer, if you'd like to take a rest from it."

"Yeah, thanks. That's always nice."

"Do you have a cell phone, sir? Most people have one to entertain them."

Mark shook his head. "I don't have a cell phone. Nobody to call."

"You have no relatives? No friends?"

"Nope."

"That sounds very sad, sir. I'm so sorry."

"Maybe I'll make some friends here."

Babs leaned forward and looked at him. "Well, you've made one so far."

Chapter Three

The dining room was huge, compared to the number of current residents in the facility. It was well lit, making Mark feel just a bit safer. As soon as she pushed him through the doors, Babs stopped and came around to the side, kneeling next to him. He looked down at her curiously.

She pointed to a group of people at a large round table near the far end of the room. "Those are your co-residents. They reside in the same hall as you, in the other rooms, you know."

"Okay." He nodded, staring at the group. There were four people at the table, three men and a woman.

"These other two tables are for the other two floors. And those over there are for the other halls on the other side of the facility."

"So do those people at my table, they here for mental problems like me?"

Babs raised her eyebrows. "Is that why you are here, Mark?"

"I thought you people already knew about the patients you bring in here."

Babs smiled, shaking her head. "I am sometimes out of the loop. But I did know that we were receiving a vet on suicide watch. That must be you."

Mark snorted. "Say the wrong thing to the wrong person one time and find yourself shipped off to a prison hospital."

Babs giggled, a strange sound that Mark didn't expect. "This is not a prison, sir, I promise."

"Call me Mark." More than anything, he wanted her to call him Mark. She gave off a warm, inviting presence and he enjoyed just having her near. He was glad she wasn't insulted when he called the place a prison. He vowed silently to be a little friendlier. He tried a smile. He knew it had to look half-hearted but he was grateful to see her laugh again.

"You don't have to worry, Mark. You won't be treated like a prisoner here, I promise."

"Well, okay, if you promise." He said. He felt stupid. He felt like that was the stupidest thing he could have said. He clenched his jaw in frustration. "Well, let's get over there already." He grunted, grasping the wheels and shoving himself forward, practically knocking Babs off balance. She hurried to stand and follow him. His cheeks were burning in embarrassment and regret. He hadn't meant to be so abrupt.

When he reached the table, Babs was by his side once again. "Hello everyone." She said with a huge grin.

"Hello, Babs!" The men lifted their hands. One of them stood up and bowed slightly from the waist.

"Ma'am." He said, winking at her.

"How are you today, Babs?" The woman asked.

"I'm doing really well today, Jenny. I want to introduce you to our newest resident, Sgt. Mark Geer. He is recovering from a spinal injury."

"Iraq?" The man who had stood up asked him as he sat. "Lybia? Afghanistan?"

"Iraq." Mark responded. "You?"

"Lybia. Got my eye shot out and took two more to the chest. Gonna have breathing problems all my life but I'm still here, aren't I? And glad of it."

"Mark, this is Jenny Garcia, Victor Tennant, David Beckett..." The man with one eye nodded in acknowledgement. "and Bob Havers. They are the residents in the rooms that surround yours."

"Thank you, Babs." He nodded up at her. Then he nodded at the group. He noticed that one place set at the table did not have a chair in front of it. He easily wheeled himself up to the table. "Convenient." He said.

"I think it would have been awfully rude if they had not set a place for you, Sgt. Geer." Jenny leaned to him and whispered dramatically, as if she was telling a secret. "They knew you were coming and had a wheelchair."

He nodded at her. "I suppose it would have been rude, Jenny."

"I hope you are comfortable in that room, Sgt. Geer." Bob spoke up. He was missing his right arm. He was short and heavy, something that must have happened after his time in service. Mark was sure he was too fatty to have been in shape to fight in combat anywhere recently. He looked like he could have been a stocky, well-built scrapper at one point but now...he was probably doing all he could to lift a jelly donut to his lips.

"I think I will be." Mark nodded. "Don't know why I wouldn't be."

"Stop being like that, Bob." Jenny slapped the air playfully in Bob's direction. She looked at Mark. "He's being a scoundrel, trying to get you freaked out, is all."

"How's that gonna happen?" Mark looked at each of the group members, confused.

Jenny raised her eyebrows. "Oh, so you don't know about that room?"

Mark closed his eyes for a moment. What did he need to know about that room? "Okay, Jenny, I'll bite. What happened in the room? Someone kill themselves? Kill someone else? Get stuck in the closet for forty years, only to be discovered living on spiders, rats and..."

"Sgt. Geer, Don't be facetious." Jenny responded, seriously. She covered her mouth with her hand and looked around as if afraid they would be heard. "That's where Jerry Wayne Hall lived."

Mark looked from one to another.

"Jenny, now you're going to be the one to put a fright in him."

Mark wasn't sure what they were talking about but if someone said he was going to be frightened one more time, he might blow his top.

To his amazement, Babs spoke up. He hadn't even realized she was still there.

"I don't think anything is going to frighten Sgt. Geer," she said, firmly, drawing the attention of the rest of the group, as well. "He volunteered for extended tours and has seen quite a lot of action."

"But you didn't tell him about that room?" Jenny shook her head. "You should have."

"What's the deal? What's up with the room?" Mark frowned at Jenny, trying to mentally drag the information from the woman. She turned her green eyes to him.

"A bad soldier lived in there."

Chapter Four

Mark was beginning to think Jenny must be simple. Why else would she be acting like a little girl? The thought made him pull back his temper somewhat. He didn't cuss out simpletons.

"What do you mean 'a bad soldier'?" he asked, forcing his voice to be more gentle.

"She means that the last guy that stayed in that room killed a bunch of people, other people that lived here. That was a long time ago, Jen, during the 80's. There's no need to bring it up now. Why would you even tell him that anyway?" Victor was shaking his head. He had a thick accent that signified to Mark he'd been raised in another country. He didn't want to hazard a guess which one but Puerto Rico came to mind right away.

"Some guy killed a bunch of people in my room back in the 80's?" He raised one eyebrow. "Okay. So is his ghost living in there now?"

"Could be." Jenny said, softly.

"Jenny!" Victor shook his head. "What's the matter with you? Just because things like that scare *you* doesn't mean it's gonna scare *him* and why would you want him to be scared anyway?"

"I don't want him to be scared."

Mark looked from one face to another, trying to figure out when he'd time-warped back to high school. He'd lost his appetite and just wanted to get away from these people. They were nuts.

His hands went to the wheels of his chair to push away but he stopped when he felt a soft hand cover one of his. He looked down and followed the arm up to Babs' smiling face.

She shook her head, leaned over and whispered, "Don't give up on them, Mark. Give them a chance. They're good people, I promise."

He instinctively breathed in her sweet strawberry scent and was sad when she pulled away. She looked at the group.

"You all behave. Show Mark a good first meal here and we'll all be happier for it. Okay?"

The group murmured in agreement and Babs walked away, laughing quietly.

At lunch and dinner, the group talked with each other as though they had been in the facility for years, rather than months or weeks. Mark was quickly able to assess that Jenny had, in fact, suffered brain damage when the military bus she had been driving was hit in the blowback from a car bomb. Her family was unable to care for her needs and she'd been placed in the facility for long-term care. She held her own, conversation-wise and would, at times, become completely coherent, as if there had never been a problem at all. Minutes later, she would revert to child-like thinking and behaviors. David, Victor and Bob were always nice to her, though they tended to put her on notice if she began to act too irrationally.

Mark liked them all.

He lay in bed that first night, thinking about their conversations. He smiled, remembering something humorous and sighed contentedly. Perhaps the facility wouldn't be so bad after all.

His eyes snapped open.

He sat up in bed. He'd heard a noise. He knew he did, even though it was dead silent. He listened closely, moving his eyes around the dark room, feeling almost blind. There was no light coming in through his window. The moon must be behind clouds. He focused on the night sky through the glass but couldn't spot even one star.

"What the hell is going on?" He thought.

He jumped when he heard the sound that had woken him ring out in the quiet once more. It was a gunshot. Definitely a gun shot. His heart sped up. He looked at his wheelchair, which was not where it was supposed to be. He liked to keep it right next to the bed, so that he could slide into it quickly. It was all the way across the room.

He heard a thump. He wondered why the sound had not happened immediately after the shot. He heard scratching sounds, as though something was being dragged across a wooden floor. His breath came and went rapidly. Chills covered his arms, running in waves up his spine, washing over his hammering heart.

He watched in stunned silence as the door to his room slowly opened, allowing light from the outer hallway to spill in. He watched as the back end of a man came through. He was dragging a body into the room. Mark could see bloody trails the dragged body was leaving behind on the floor.

He opened his mouth but could not speak. His door stayed open, letting in the light. Now he saw that the room was littered with bodies...at least three others besides the one the man was dragging in.

Rage filled him, extinguishing his confusion and concern. He wanted to leap out of the bed, grab the murderer and snap his pathetic neck.

His hands balled up into fists and his jaw clenched. If he had superhuman powers, if he only had the use of his legs...

The man turned and stared directly at him, causing him to freeze in place. The man was dressed in the green uniform of the Vietnam war era. Mark instantly knew who he was. The symbol on the side of this shirt indicated he was a Sergeant. Sgt. Hall approached until he was leaned over, his face mere inches from Mark's.

"I did my part, buddy," he grumbled in low voice. *"Now it's your turn."*

Chapter Five

Mark sat up in bed, suddenly awake. The sun was peeking in through the window. He looked around frantically but the room was empty other than him, no bodies on the floor, no blood trailing in through the door, no Vietnam vet trying to terrify him.

He could still see Sgt. Hall, his face so close to him, appearing so very real. He could hear the words he'd growled out. *"Now it's your turn."*

What could that mean? Mark's career of killing the enemy was over. He couldn't walk. He would be sent stateside to live a miserable, unhappy life alone until he finally died.

His wheelchair was next to his bed, as it was supposed to be. He pulled himself into it and settled in, trying to get comfortable. He grabbed a pillow from his bed and put it behind his back. Sighing, he went to the bathroom to brush his teeth and get ready for the day.

Everything in the bathroom was eye level for him. As soon as he entered the room, he felt cold and knew something was wrong. It only took a glance in the mirror to see what it was. His reflection was not his own. It was the face of Sergeant Jerry Hall. He pushed himself immediately back out of the room, rolling backwards so quickly he bumped into the bed. His breathing was loud and anxious. Was he still dreaming?

He looked around.

He couldn't be. It was too real. It *was* real.

You think you can rid of me that easy? He heard whispered into his ear. He turned sharply but no one was beside him. You can't see me, you fool. You are me. It's time to do what you know you have to do.

"Get out of my head!" Mark leaned forward, holding both fists up against the sides of his head. "Get out! Get out of my head!"

Beating yourself up isn't going to make me go away. Mark hated the sound of the ghostly voice, sweeping through his mind like hot steam.

You need to do this. These people are responsible for all the bad things that have happened to you in your life. They need to pay.

"That's insane! You're making me insane! You're going to make me look crazy to all these people. Get out of my head. Leave me alone!" He shoved his chair in the direction of the door. He wanted to leave the room immediately.

The chair made it to about two feet from the door before the wheels froze in place. He pushed on them as hard as he could but even with his muscles bulging, the wheels would no longer move.

He had been trained to fight an enemy...an enemy he could see. How was he supposed to fight one that he could not see, one that was embedded in his mind? His mind raced with memories that weren't his, he could see military authority figures in front of his eyes, yelling at him. He could feel the resentment Sgt. Hall let brew deep inside of him, welling up until the young man could no longer take it. He let out his anger in an explosive way, slaughtering the other four residents in the wing Mark was now staying.

If he had his way, Mark knew Sgt. Hall would take over his body. If that happened, everyone in the facility was in danger. But what could he do?

You aren't going out of this room. Not until you are ready to do what needs to be done.

"I will never do it." Mark spoke through clenched teeth. "I will never do what you want me to do. I will leave this room. I will get out and tell them..."

His mind whirled. What would he tell them? That a ghost was haunting him? That it would force him to do unspeakable things, slaughter not the enemy but the innocent?

He couldn't do that without putting himself in more trouble. They might restrain him. Keep him under constant supervision, no matter where he was or what he was doing.

You don't have a choice.

"If I do what you want, they will put me on death row. I do have a choice. I can either kill innocent people or sacrifice my life."

No one will sacrifice themselves for others. You aren't so noble so don't kid yourself.

"I'm not trying to be noble." Mark leaned forward and grabbed the pillow from behind his back. He threw it on the ground in front of him and shoved himself out of the chair. "I'm just not going to kill innocent people."

You joined the army so you could kill people.

"I joined so I could kill the enemy. Every enemy. No innocent." Mark pulled himself over the thin carpeting toward the door after landing safely on the pillow. He wasn't sure how strong he was, after more than six months of being confined to a wheelchair. He wasn't sure if his bones would break. He tried sliding the pillow along under him and was finding the entire thing incredibly difficult to do. He looked up at the doorknob. It looked a million miles away, even though it was lower than regular doorknobs.

He reached up to grasp the doorknob, pulling his torso up from the floor. He felt something solid press hard against his chest, slamming him back down to the ground. He tried again and again, but the force would not let him reach the doorknob.

I told you, the voice sent painful anger coursing through his body. *The only way you're going out there, buddy, is to do what you need to do.*

Chapter Six

Frustration and anger were mounting in his mind. Mark couldn't move. All he could think about was keeping the sergeant from possessing his body somehow. He wished he had some salt or something, anything that the many ghost and demon hunters he'd seen on TV used to get rid of ghosts. He could hear chuckling, which fueled his rage even more, like throwing lighter fluid on a burning fire.

Those people out there aren't innocent. They might not have done something to you directly but they are part of the reason you're stuck here.

"That's stupid. That's insane. You don't know what you're talking about." Mark had grown weary trying to open the door. He crawled back to his chair and pulled himself up in it. A plan was forming in his mind. He didn't know whether the ghost sergeant could hear his thoughts so he tried to think in a scattered manner, only letting himself glimpse the seed of the plan. He wanted to help it grow without the sergeant catching on to what he planned to do.

He rolled his chair to the bathroom once again and went in. His heart was pounding hard as he tried not to focus on Sgt. Hall in the mirror. He reached up and pulled on the mirror, hoping beyond hope it was a medicine cabinet. When it came open, he frantically searched the small shelves for what he wanted. Relief flooded him when he saw it. He reached up and pulled the straight razor down.

Looks like you're all ready to go.

"I'm not using this on those innocent people out there." He pictured the other members of his wing, Jenny with her child-like mind, David with the one eye, constantly doing Popeye impressions that were too on point for his own good, Victor with his thick accent and Bob with the one arm, proudly proclaiming he would never be held in handcuffs again. He knew they were good people. He suspected the people Sgt. Hall had killed were just as innocent.

No one is innocent, Sgt. Geer. You need to do what's right. You need to end their misery. They are just as unhappy as you are. They have been mutilated by this world. They need you to end it for them so they can go on to a better place.

"That's not my call. If God didn't want them here, they wouldn't be here."

You can't possibly believe that crap. Take the straight razor and do what's right for those people. You think you care about them? If you really did, you'd be following my call to action right now and we wouldn't be debating it.

"Nope. You aren't going to convince me." He left the bathroom and moved his chair in such a way that it bumped the side of his bed. When it did, he slipped his hand under the side railing that was used to help him get in and out of it. There was a small button on the side of the metal part of the bed. He pressed it once and let go, hoping once would be enough to summon a nurse or someone to his room.

He pulled the straight razor open and pressed the edge of it against his wrist.

Don't do that. He could tell Sgt. Hall was not happy to see what he was planning to do. He rested the edge of the blade there for a prolonged period of time, his heart thumping. Where was the nurse? Surely someone saw his signal. Thoughts buzzed through his mind. What if the light outside his room didn't turn on? What if there was no one at the nurse's desk or the receptionist desk? What if the doctor wasn't there that early in the morning?

What are you doing? Don't be so stupid!

"I figure if they find another vet has killed himself in this room, they will shut it off to more patients."

Don't be a martyr. They aren't worth it!

"They don't deserve to die. Not at my hand. I won't kill them."

To his utter relief, there was a quick knock on his door before it swung open and Babs put her head in. She already looked concerned but when her eyes dropped to the straight razor in his hand, she leapt into the room and grabbed him, pulling the razor away from his skin.

"What are you doing, Mark? What are you thinking? You can't do this!" She went on, berating him in a kind and concerned voice, folding the straight razor and sliding it into her pocket. She went from terror to confusion, staring down at him. He'd put up no fight.

"I will do it again if I'm not let out of this room." He said. He could hear Sgt. Hall cussing both of them out but straightened what was left of his spine, squaring his shoulders and looking defiant. "I refuse to stay in this room another minute."

Babs leaned forward, her voice gentle as she spoke. "All you had to do was ask for a transfer, Mark. You don't have to kill yourself to be moved."

He smiled at her. He pulled in a deep breath of sweet strawberry scent. He glanced over his shoulder with a sneer as Babs pushed his chair out of the room.

In the end, those in authority decided to move Mark to a completely different facility, where the other patients were not strictly military but were there for spinal injuries. Now everyone he was around was in a wheelchair. The men had formed a basketball team and spent a lot of time training each other how to do common things without letting the wheelchair hold them back.

He made several friends just on the first day, openly expressing his love for basketball, confessing he'd been sure he would never play another day in his life. His new friends let him know that was definitely not the case. He went to bed the first day feeling open, free and happy for the first time in nearly a year.

As he fell asleep, he felt a cool breeze blow over him.

His eyes snapped open.

He heard a faint, low chuckling drift through the air toward his ears.

Sorry, buddy, he heard. *I told you ya wouldn't get rid of me that easy. It's your turn to do what you need to do, sergeant. And this time, there's gonna be a lot more bodies to pile up.*

Mark squeezed his eyes shut, fighting instant rage, gripping the pillow under his head until his knuckles were white.

"No," he said. "No, no, no, no!"

THE ACCUSED

EMILY MOON

Sebastian Tomlinson rubbed his temples. If police sirens at dark thirty weren't enough, he had to witness his son's arrest. He'd had many cases as a defense lawyer where something like this had happened: a child would be arrested for being a witness before they could testify, and sometimes, the police wouldn't let them talk before getting a lawyer. He could understand that his son was at the scene of the murder; the girl was his girlfriend, after all.

What he couldn't understand was that the police thought he was the murderer. Other than a shoe that had been lost in a frenzy to get away and his sweatshirt, there was no evidence. Of course his prints were all over her hands and waist. She had been strangled, the police told him, and the killer had used some sort of cloth and gloves. They would not be able to pull prints.

As Sebastian slugged through the evidence file, his stomach dropped. There seemed to be an air tight case against Patrick. He was the only person that could be placed at the crime scene. The fact that his shoe and sweatshirt were at the scene corroborated that. Everything else belonged to Rani Hutchinson, the young girl that was killed.

Her purse had been flung into the alleyway, and police suspected she had followed after a harsh shove; the bruises on her back indicated some sort of hard push. They also suspected that Rani had been attacked from behind; there were purple splotches around her mouth that indicated a hand pressed against her mouth to shut her up.

Once the deed had been done, she had been flung aside like a rag doll. Her skull smashed in, and the medical examiner's report noted that she had received a beating before being killed. Various bruises and stages of clotting were found on her chest and back from small, deliberate cuts and punches.

The worst damage had been done to her face. Her eye swelled up before she died, and someone had decided to take inspiration from the Black Dahlia – Elizabeth Short – and cut her mouth open on the sides.

From the blood trails on her cheeks and neck, it had been done when she was alive.

However, the strongest piece of evidence the police had against Patrick was that he had bloody hands. The blood test revealed it to be Rani's blood. Patrick protested that he had been trying to save his girlfriend, but had run to get help. The police had picked him up while he was on the run.

Now, two weeks into the trial, he was beginning to lose hope. His son acted out in court earlier that day, claiming he could see Rani's ghost. The judge had laughed at him, but adjourned the court for the day. Sebastian had watched helplessly as his son had been restrained and returned to the waiting area to calm down. He wasn't allowed to go out until the officers were sure that he had calmed down.

Upon arriving in the small holding cell that Patrick had been escorted to after calming down, Sebastian sighed.

"Patrick...I can't help you If you insist we have it all wrong." He tried to keep an even tone. "Are you feeling alright?"

"I'm fine." The bitter words stung. "I didn't kill Rani, but she knows who did." His tone gave way to a softer one, as if he was unable to stomach the idea. "She knows who did it and because you refuse to believe me, her murderer will not be brought to justice."

"Son, I know you didn't do it. In your case, however, you simply cannot be going off the rails like that." He took a firmer tone as he began to reprimand his son. "Are you pretending to see her ghost so that you can get off the hook as insane? Let me tell you something: that defense strategy will land you in a mental institution for longer than you want." He'd seen people try to defend themselves with it all the time, usually faking it until they made it and escaping later on. Some made it out, but the majority ended up institutionalized and actually going insane.

"I know, dad!" Patrick yelled, which was rare for him. The usually even-tempered kid fled in the face of jail. Tears began to run down his face. "You don't think I already know that? I'm telling the truth. Why don't you believe me?" The words felt like a slap to the face.

Sebastian blinked slowly. How could his son believe that he didn't believe him?

Then, he frowned. His words had not been the best for the situation.

"Patrick..." He sat down beside his son on the little bench and hugged him tight. "I know it's difficult to lose a loved one." With a gentle hand, he wiped the tears off his son's face. "This case hasn't been easy for anyone. Rani's parents aren't sure what to believe. I'm trying my best to defend you. The state wants to see you sent to prison for life." He sighed. "Did you really see her ghost?"

The young one nodded slowly as his hiccups and sobs slowed down. As he calmed down, the lawyer sighed softly. He wanted to believe his son, he really did, but...something about the timing and the reason threw him off. Why would his son start *now*? Had the police missed something and he was trying to draw attention to it? Or was he really going insane and the insanity defense was their only shot at keeping him from going to jail for life?

"Let's go home. I'll make some spaghetti, and we can talk about this over dinner. How's that sound?" With a soft tone, he managed to make his son smile a little. Rani's death had destroyed him, but he was determined not to let his son destroy his life over it. Instead, he made sure that he got up every day, and that he did something productive each day – even if that was simply making his bed.

He helped Patrick up before escorting him out to their car. His son's license had been suspended until the trial was over, so Sebastian had to take him everywhere. The state was afraid that, given the opportunity, he would run. He had gotten them to give him custody of his son during the trial, but with a couple of hitches.

The first was that neither of them could leave the state. The second was the aforementioned license suspension. The final hitch was that

Patrick had to be in the home between the hours of ten in the evening to seven in the morning.

The ride home was rather quiet. He focused on the road, but his mind wandered. Now that he thought about it, the past two weeks had been difficult for his son in a variety of ways. Rani was dead. Her father blamed him for it. Her mother was too depressed to do anything.

Patrick had spent the first few days after his arrest locked away in his room. He wouldn't talk to anyone – the police, the counselors, not even his own father. After the initial grief passed, he had become determined to find Rani's killer. Since then, he had spent every hour he could outside in the city, searching the area around where she had been killed and other areas they frequented to find a clue.

As far as he was away, the search had come up empty.

"Dad?" His son broke the silence about half way home.

"Yes?" He gave a side eye glance to show that he was listening.

"Could we go to Rani's favorite restaurant tonight instead?" His request caught him off guard. "Her birthday is tomorrow, and I...I don't want to do it tomorrow."

He glanced down at the clock. It was only six PM.

"As long as you promise we'll be done before nine." He smiled a little. "I'd hate to see you busted for breaking bail rules." The humor broke the ice and he saw his son smile again. He hadn't seen that smile for two weeks; to see it again meant the world to Sebastian. If he could get him to smile again, maybe it was worth listening to his son.

However, the conversation would have to wait until they returned home.

"I realize that means we have to wait. Can we push the conversation away until the day after tomorrow?" He watched as Patrick bit his lip. The motion was one of nerves; his son always did it the day of a big test or when he was getting ready to ask Rani out on another date. It was adorable in a typical 18 year old man way, but left his lips incredibly chapped.

"Stop biting your lip, Patrick. Yes, it can wait. May I ask where you plan to go tomorrow?"

"Rani's grave." He sighed. "We had plans for tomorrow..." Hearing that made Sebastian's heart sink. "I had a ring, dad. Why would I kill her if I was planning to propose tomorrow?"

"How did you manage to sneak a ring past me?" He furrowed his eyebrows. He had been watching his son for two weeks.

"I bought it the day before she was murdered." His voice quivered. "I love Rani, dad. I love her so much, and now she's gone!"

"I know, Patrick. I know." He patted his son's shoulder as he spoke. "I didn't realize you were so serious. She was turning 18, right?"

"Yes." He sighed wearily. "She was too sweet to stand up for herself. Please dad, you have to trust me." He begged again, looking him in the eyes with tears ready to storm his face as if there were someone hostage.

"I want to trust you, but it is so difficult to when everyone wants me to give up on the case. To convince you to plead guilty." He sighed. "I love you, Patrick. I do, but some people believe this is a lost cause. Especially after your little outburst today." Instead of turning right, he continued straight to honor his son's wishes. "Please, trust me."

"Will you come with me tomorrow? To Rani's grave?"

"I think that's a wonderful idea. Why don't you bring the ring and we can set up a small shrine at her grave?" He tried to alleviate the pain of losing his girlfriend somehow. Patrick nodded and tried not to cry again.

The rest of the ride to the restaurant was silent. Patrick's spirits seemed to be lifting, and maybe, just maybe, he was coming out of the insanity that had gripped him in court.

By the time they arrived at the restaurant, Sebastian began to wonder if his son really had killed Rani. An insanity plea would keep him from serving any real hard time, and if he was so inclined, he could use the temporary insanity defense. It wouldn't land him in an institution for long, but it'd be long enough to convince the court that he had recovered.

Patrick would know this; he had been interested in law as a kid. He would read the books Sebastian owned for hours on end and ask him to define the legal terms in simple terms for him. Happily, he'd obliged for the less gruesome terms. This included the temporary insanity defense.

He put the thought aside to enjoy a dinner with his son. There would be no talk of murder, of prison, or even of Rani for one night. He made sure to make his son promise him that much. They could talk about anything else, but for one night, he wanted it to be like Rani's death was not the freshest thing on his mind.

As dinner progressed, he watched his son carefully. Half way through the meal, he stood up rigidly.

"Rani!" He yelled her name, and ran after nothing. Sebastian sighed, and quickly paid for the meal. Then, he ran after his son.

"Patrick! Get back here!" He was too old to do this. Chasing after people was the police department's forte, not his. For the sake of his son's safety, however, he pressed on despite the panting. Each step closed the gap a little bit, but his son ran track. He didn't stand a chance of catching up to him.

So, he decided to see if he could cut him off. He took a short cut to reach the grave yard first. As he suspected, he did arrive first. When Patrick arrived, his eyes had become bloodshot. He was panting heavily, and tears ran down his face.

"Rani..." He tried to yell again, but the sobs were too much. His son fell to his knees, and began to sob. "I'm sorry."

He wasn't sure what to do. Though it was only eight PM now, he knew word would make it to the police. Once that happened, there was no telling what kind of restrictions they would lay on Patrick. It was entirely possible that they would actually arrest him. That possibility made him act.

Sebastian slowly walked towards his son. He was sobbing too loudly to hear the crunching grass and fallen leaves of the Halloween season. Until he was right there, Patrick didn't know who was coming.

"Patrick?" He spoke, interrupting the silence. "Are you alright?" He put a hand on his son's shoulder, trying desperately to get some response from him. "Patrick?"

"Go away." His son's voice came out in a strangled sob. "Go away."

"Patrick, you know I can't." He sat down beside him on the ground. The ground mushed up underneath him from all the rain that had fallen in the past couple of days. "I can leave you alone, but I have to stay nearby." He tried to find the words.

"You don't trust me, and you won't listen. So go away." The words stung him. How could his son think he wouldn't listen?

"Son..." He was at a loss for words. "Please..."

"I said go away!" Now, he visibly pulled away from him. "I'll be back by ten."

"I can't leave you alone. I'm worried about you, Rick." He used a nickname instead of his full name. "When did you first see Rani's ghost?" Though every bone in him screamed not to entertain his son's fantasy, it was entirely possible that he was telling the truth – especially if the scene in the restaurant had been some sort of way to get his attention. Luckily for them, no cops were coming to find them yet.

"Yesterday, in court." He sniffled, looking up from his lap, half in disbelief. "She was just...sitting by her parents. I don't think she saw me."

"Is that why you didn't freak out yesterday?" He managed to keep his voice even. This was a subject close to his son's heart, and he didn't want to say something that would make him close up again.

Patrick simply nodded, trying to find the words to express how he felt.

"Why did you freak out this morning?" He couldn't stop himself from asking. The tender moment pushed his son too far and tears began to roll.

"She loved me." The three little words came in a choked sob as he tried to come to grips with what had happened. "That's why I freaked out. She loved me, dad." He closed his eyes as the sobs came harder, leaving him unable to speak.

Without a word, Sebastian wrapped his arms around his son, pulling him into a hug. He didn't ask how he knew that. He didn't ask why he knew she loved him. Instead, he simply let his son cry. Over the past two weeks, he hadn't had a chance to properly mourn his girlfriend. He'd been prodded. He'd been questioned. He had even had his room searched to find bloody fabric (which only turned up on the clothes he had been wearing at the time of Rani's murder, but that's beside the point). Even worse, a bandana had turned up a couple of days before covered in blood.

With Patrick's finger prints all over it.

He tried not to think about it, but now that he was, he remembered something odd. Patrick's nose had wrinkled up upon seeing the bandana. His nose wrinkled when he was thinking, and it had wrinkled more than usual. He'd been thinking hard.

A sniffle caught Sebastian's attention. He looked down to find his son sniffling, trying to calm down. He rubbed his back a little more, trying to offer some inkling of support. The way his son felt was not new to him; he'd felt the same way when his wife passed in childbirth.

"C-Can we...go home...?" Patrick managed to say something. He nodded, and helped his son off the muddy ground.

"The car is back at the restaurant, but I can get it after I get you home." Instead of focusing on making sure his car was not towed, he put the priority on getting his son home. Making sure his son got home put the priority on his well-being, and it felt like the right thing to do in this situation. After all, if he listened to his son, maybe it was possible that he could bring him back to earth. Or at the very least, convince him that he wasn't seeing Rani's ghost.

"Th...Thanks dad." He hiccupped again, but managed a smile.

"Take your sleeping pill when we get home, please." He reminded his son to take his medicine. "Maybe you're a little sleep deprived."

Before Patrick could protest, he yawned. With a nod, all protest ended before it could even begin. Sebastian smiled a little, and walked with his son, one arm wrapped around his shoulders and the other swinging lightly to his side as they walked.

"Thanks...for listening." Now somewhat calm, his son was able to speak without hiccupping. He smiled and nodded, stating that he was happy his son felt that he could be a confidante.

They arrived home, and he walked Patrick up to his room. He watched as the medicine was taken, and his son lay down in the bed. Within minutes, he was out cold, snoring lightly.

Sebastian smiled, and pulled the door softly closed behind him as he left his son's room. Instead of going to get his car immediately, he replaced the bottle of sleeping pills in the pantry. However, he noticed something off.

So, he opened the bottle of pills. There were two kinds of pills in the bottle. One was a circular white pill. The other was an oddly shaped blue pill. Grabbing his phone, he managed to take photos of the pills. His son's sleeping pills were circular and white, but to be safe, he was going to have them both tested.

Careful not to drop the pills, he walked towards the pantry. He had to grab two small plastic bags – one for each pill. One of his friends worked in a chemical lab and owed him a favor. With the resolution to get the pills to him before Patrick could go out of the house tomorrow, Sebastian labelled the two bags with a permanent marker. One was labelled 'pill A' and the other was labelled 'pill B'.

Something about it stank like fish.

However, there was nothing he could do but give his friend a call at nine thirty at night. When the name Emilia Thatcher lit up on his phone, he was almost positive something had broken in the case.

"Hey, Em. I was about to call you."

"I found traces of a drug on Rani's skin from the blood sample they took. It must've come from the killer's gloves."

"I have some pills I need you to run. We might find the match."

"Pills? Where did you get pills?"

"I think someone switched out Rick's sleeping pills with something to cause hallucinations. The pills were refilled, and we picked them up yesterday. Yesterday is also the first time he saw Rani's ghost." He waited with baited breath for his friend to say something. Instead, a silence set in that spanned almost five minutes.

"Bring them over." Em eventually broke the silence. "I've got nothing better to do, and if it means Rick's innocent, I'm more than willing to help."

"You're a lifesaver, Emilia. I'll be over in a few minutes; I have to go get my car from the restaurant..."

"You have a story to tell me while the drugs are sampled." Before he could protest, the line was dead. Laughing to himself, he shook his head and quickly wrote a note for Patrick, in case he woke up before he came back.

With the note posted on his son's bedroom door, and his son still sound asleep, he began to walk back towards the restaurant. Hopefully, his car hadn't been towed yet, and he could get it home before the restaurant realized he had left it.

He arrived in time to see them hooking it up to the tow truck.

"I am so sorry about this, sir." Sebastian sighed, rubbing his temples again. "Can I pay the fine and we can forget about this?"

"You're the one who chased after his son, right?" The night manager was getting ready to leave, but got out of his car. He nodded slowly. "I didn't realize you had not taken your car. Give him his car, guys. No fine for him, either."

"Thank you, sir." He turned towards the night manager. "You have no idea what a day I've had."

"I think I have some idea." The guy smiled. "Take care, and I hope your son is feeling alright."

"Thank you, again, sir." He couldn't help but smile widely as the tow truck attendants took the rigging off his car. "I'm sorry about this, guys." He apologized once more to them before getting into his car. With the keys in hand, he was able to start it and drive towards Emilia's.

He hadn't seen Emilia in almost three months. She had probably changed the color and style of her hair, and probably had a nose ring now; she had always thought about getting one and was working up the courage to get it.

Would her hair be pink or blue or maybe purple? Would she have picked a more neutral color this time, or stay with the wild colors?

Shaking his head, he paid attention to the road. Luckily, it wasn't a long drive to her house, and he arrived soon enough. His curiosity would soon be calmed.

Without thinking, he simply entered as he always did.

"Emilia! I'm here!"

"Basement!" It didn't surprise him to hear her voice yell to him. She seemed unfazed by the fact that he had simply walked in. With a smile, he began to walk towards the basement steps.

In her basement, she had set up a chemistry lab. Here, she did pro-bono work for those who couldn't afford to have an actual chemical lab test it. She even did free or discounted blood test for those who were worried but couldn't see a doctor. The best part was that she was completely accredited; doctors had to honor what she found, even though she made very little to nothing off the people she did the tests for. Her heart of gold was worth every penny that was spent on her work.

He pushed the door at the bottom of the stairs further open. To his surprise, she was sitting down instead of standing at her desk.

"This is quite a change." He smiled. "Oh. Nice hair." Today, her hair was a teal green color with purple highlights.

"Thank you." Emilia turned around. He saw her right ear covered in multiple piercings, while her left had only one piercing – where everyone had pierced – and a cuff. Her lip ring was out, but there was a nose ring sitting pretty on her nose. "Yes, I did get the nose piercing. Two months ago."

"Nice." He smiled. "So, here are the pills. I think the white one is his regular prescription, and I have no idea what the blue one is." As he spoke, he pulled the pills out. "You know the name of his prescription, right?"

"Yup. These two boogers should be analyzed in two, maybe two and a half, hours." She smiled and took the two bags. "Thank you for putting them in separate bags. Have the two touched?"

"They were in the pill bottle together." He shrugged. "Probably, but I thought it best to prevent any further cross-contamination."

"I appreciate that, but I will probably find traces on each of them." She laughed a little and began to prep the samples. "How's Rick doing, anyway?"

"Rani's death has been difficult on him." He sighed. "He was the last person to see her alive, according to the police. What drug did you find on in the blood?" He made an attempt to change the topic. While it wasn't entirely subtle, he didn't really care at this point.

"LSD." Emilia replied off-handedly while she was setting a solution. "It's very odd; Rani is one of the cleanest women I know. Same goes for Rick, man-wise, at least. I don't he would've spiked her drink, and since it was a large trace, it's too large to have been in her system. Even weirder: the blood in her feet, where we pulled the other blood sample, had no LSD."

"Would you be willing to run a blood test on Rick?" Pieces of a puzzle began to turn in his head. "And fingerprint the bottle? The police have all but given up on trying to find another suspect, and they keep telling me that the case is a lost cause." Another sigh escaped his lips before he began to chew his lip.

"Thankfully I have your fingerprints and Rick's in my database for elimination purposes." With this, Emilia turned to him. "Well, the pills are running. We have a while before it dings."

"Thank you, so much, Em." He smiled. "I'll run home and get the bottle." Then, he looked at the time. "You'll have to wait until tomorrow to run Patrick's blood test." When he looked up, he was met by furrowed brows.

"Why?"

"Part of the reason he's not in jail is because they set a curfew – between ten PM and seven AM, he has to be in the house. It's too close to his curfew."

"Is he still awake?" Emilia cocked her head to the side. "If he is, you could draw some blood. Did he take a pill already?"

"Yes. He's already t-" He was cut off when his phone rang. "I should get that." He picked up and walked a few steps away. Emilia turned back to her computer.

"Dad..." Patrick's voice came through the phone. "I see her again. She wants me to follow her."

"Rick, stay there." He used a firm, but calm, tone. "I think I know what's going on."

"Hurry." His son sounded frightened, upset even. He sighed. The line went dead before he could try to comfort his son.

"That was Rick, wasn't it?" Emilia didn't need to turn from her computer. "Can I run and grab the stuff, and draw some blood? I need someone here to watch the computer."

"It'll only take us half an hour or so. I need to be there too." He thought. It usually took him ten minutes to drive to her house. "It might not even take that long. Can we do it together?"

"Wait, I have a solution." The quick thinker that she was, she managed to make a live feed to her phone of the computer and the station she had set up to test the pills. Then, she grabbed the supplies she needed to transport a few samples of blood. "Now we can go. Ride together?"

"But of course." He smiled. After making sure she had enough data left to make it to his house and back while watching the feed, she strode right on up the steps. Ever the confident one, she left him half in the dust. He laughed to himself, and followed her up the stairs.

If his hunch proved right, then his son was innocent, *and* sane.

"How much would be in his system if he takes one a day?"

"He takes it right before he goes to sleep, so I'd say a pretty significant amount right now." Emilia's response was pretty sound. "He might have some leftover from yesterday, but I doubt it. It also depends on what the composition of those pills are, and which pills he had."

"I think he's managed to get two blue ones, but I'm not sure. There were fewer white pills than blue ones." Sebastian furrowed his brows. "Is it possible they put the white ones in to pass it off as full of white pills?"

"Possible, but unlikely. They probably ran out of the blue ones to spike your son's medicine with." The analysis of the situation made sense. If they had meant to spike the medicine, they would've wanted to remove all trace of his normal medicine.

By now, they had gotten into the car and were half way to his house. The conversation stalled, but he didn't mind. Instead, she was watching the feed as he drove.

They arrived at his house. The moment they entered, Sebastian knew something was off. The house was a mess, and Patrick – the poor young man – was shivering in a corner. He held his hand up to stop

Emilia from approaching, but it was too late. She approached him, and took his hand softly. The young man was startled, but didn't lash back against it. Instead, he looked up and tried to form a sentence.

"Help…" The only word that came from his son's mouth broke his heart.

"She's here to help you, Patrick." He spoke calmly. "Can Emilia draw some blood?" With slow speech, he made sure his son understood what was happening. Emilia held up her gear, causing Patrick to nod slowly.

As he always did, he looked away as she poked the needle into his vein. When she had it ready to go, he looked at it. He loved to watch the blood flow into the little vials.

"See? Not so bad." She smiled as he watched the blood. "How are you, Rick?" The young man sniffled.

"I miss Rani." The three words were softly spoken. In the silence of the home, he could hear them clearly. Turning to face his son, he noticed that there were tears on his cheeks. However, he pushed that aside for long enough to grab the pill bottle.

Once he had the pill bottle in a plastic bag, he quickly hurried to console his son. Wrapping an arm around his shoulders, he let his son cry. The pain was still fresh, and despite the many breakdowns he'd already had, the tears continued to come. With his free hand, he stroked his son's head as Emilia did her business with the blood.

As she got ready to pull the needle out, Patrick began to fall asleep again. Either his medicine was kicking in again, or he was simply exhausted. Whatever was causing him to fall asleep was beside the point.

"There we go. All better." She gently pressed the bandage against his skin and made sure it was secure. "Are you going to put him to bed, or let him sleep on the couch?"

"I'll let him sleep on the couch. As long as he stays in the home, he's alright." With that, he gently picked his son up. For an 18 year old, he wasn't that heavy. Setting him gently on the couch, he made sure not to put pressure on the arm she had drawn blood from. He'd done that once and Patrick had had a large bruise for a week.

When he was sure he was fast asleep, he left another short note before following Emilia out to the car. She pulled the feed up again, and sat in the back this time. He let her do as she pleased, and drove the ten minutes back to her place.

"Anything yet?" He spoke up cautiously about halfway through the boring night drive.

"Nothing. Looks like there's still half an hour or so on the run, which is odd. We were only gone for about twenty minutes."

"Maybe you already have a sample in storage?" This had never happened before. However, they were both stumped.

"Even then, it usually takes longer than fifty or so minutes." She seemed to be going off into her own little world.

A set of screeching tires startled him. Before he could slam the breaks, metal crunched and he jarred against the door. He hit his head, and the space around him began to spin. Emilia passed out. With eyes half opened, he watched as someone opened the door and began to search her. When he found the smart phone, tossed halfway into the back seat, he hesitated. The feed was still playing.

"Crap." The newcomer spoke one word. Pinned in, he couldn't do much. However, Sebastian felt like he recognized that voice.

Slowly, the man began to work his way towards him. He didn't think to see if he was awake; had he caused the crash?

"Where is that stupid bottle?" He continued to mutter to himself. When he couldn't find it, Sebastian found him getting right on top of him to search his pinned body. He cared to look at his face, and noticed that he was still awake. He muttered something else and hit Sebastian's head hard with a detached headrest.

When his eyes opened again, he was in a hospital room. Emilia was in the bed beside him, hooked up to a support system.

To the side, he noticed Patrick. An officer was standing outside the door, but Patrick was fast asleep on the chair.

As he tried to sit up, he moaned. The crash had bent and broken him more than he thought. His moan woke his son up.

"Dad..." The sleepy voice made him curious. "Are you alright?"

"I've...been better." His throat was scratched up and speech was difficult. "Emilia?"

"Coma." Patrick rubbed his eyes. "The poor woman was hit hard on the head in the crash. However, there was a man on top of you when the police arrived. He had Emilia's phone in hand."

"He could've..."

"That's what the police thought too." His son tried to keep him from speaking too much. "They ran his blood and found a rather low amount of LSD in it. The police even looked at Emilia's results and ran the samples she had taken of my blood. It was the same LSD as the stuff that was in the guy's blood. The evidence was enough to hold him."

"Is he...?"

"They're searching his house. I know they found a fake pharmacy badge and ID." The pieces slowly began to come together. "They think he switched a majority of my pills so that it'd be harder to pin point what was going on."

"Is it all out of your system?"

"They made sure to give me a lot of water to help flush it out. I'm still seeing things, but they're almost positive I'm off the hook now." He managed a smile. "Thank you dad. Without you...none of this would have happened. I'd be going to jail."

He reached his hand out and took his son's hand in his.

"Rani would be proud of you." Despite how much it hurt to talk, he continued. "You never gave up looking."

His son's eyes teared up, and he simply couldn't hold it in any more. He hugged him tight, sobbing. Sebastian managed to hug him back, trying to calm him down a little bit.

It wasn't long before a police officer came in.

"We finished the search of Mr. Jenson's home." He seemed to be unsure of what to say. "He had dated Rani before you met her, Mr. Tomlinson. It seems he didn't take the breakup well and one thing led to another. There are records of him calling her multiple times in the week leading up to her murder. We even found LSD pills in her purse, most likely a gift from him that she meant to throw away."

"Is he the killer?"

"At the moment, it's too soon to tell. It's looking more and more likely. Of course, we do ask that you stay in state until we have enough evidence to actually arrest him." Now, the officer turned to Sebastian. "We think he crashed into you on purpose. He wanted to wipe the bottle; we're running prints now using Emilia's database and ours. We do expect to see your prints and his on the bottle, as well as your son's."

With that, the police officer left the room.

It didn't take long for the police to crack down on the evidence and find what they needed to issue an arrest. Mr. Jenson admitted that he had killed Rani in an act of passionate rage, but it was not enough to save him from conviction.

Patrick was declared a free man. With nothing left to lose, the day he was acquitted of the charges, he placed the ring on Rani's grave.

"I love you, Rani."